The *Longest* Feather

For further information:
djclpoetry@cableone.net

Book design by:
Arbor Books, Inc.
19 Spear Road, Suite 301
Ramsey, NJ 07446
www.arborbooks.com

Printed in The United State of America

The Longest Feather
Denis Trom
1. Title 2. Author 3. Suspense/Thriller

Library of Congress Control Number: 2008909458

ISBN 10: 0-9821906-0-3
ISBN 13: 978-0-9821906-0-9

The *Longest* Feather

A Novel Experience

Denis Trom

Sapphire Press

Acknowledgments

This novel was written in appreciation of my loving wife, Corliss, who has encouraged me to write and has tolerated all that goes with my creativity flares. I acknowledge we are stewards of all things great and small, including Othello, our best friend, and Mort, our spoiled-rotten cat. I dedicate this book to our beloved son, Todd, and our grandchildren, Passion Marie, Hunter Denis and Kaelinn Michelle, in hope that they follow their dreams. I honor my parents and my siblings, Larry, Bruce and Cheryl, with whom I share family. I cherish the wonderful friends, acquaintances, and fellow employees I have met. And to the one from whom all blessings and this gift flows, I humbly give thanks.

1

It was *finally* Saturday morning and the start of another weekend. Mickey threw the covers back and leaped onto the wooden floor, careful not to step on Othello. He peered out his bedroom window, across the golden field. The beards of wheat were moving to and fro as if stroked by invisible hands. The sun was peeking over the dilapidated barn and erasing shadows of haze in its path. He knew Mom was cooking breakfast as he could see the smoke from their chimney swirl about the yard, and he could smell the bacon.

Mickey smiled. This was the day he had been dreaming of. And he knew he'd better get moving if he had any hope of being the first one in line.

"Mom," *he* hollered. "Mom, where is my shoe?"

Summer seemed so far off and so long ago. Mickey couldn't have cared less that the summer had evaporated and that he was back in school. As a matter of fact, he liked school, and this was the season he had been anxiously awaiting. To him there were just two seasons: summer and hunting. Summer was a waste of time; he preferred hunting season better. He was a hunter and everyone knew you couldn't hunt in the summer.

"Look behind the washer. Othello likes to hide her bones there," his mother replied warmly, suggesting she was part of the caper.

Othello's bark was worse than her bite, but if she ever thought someone would hurt one of the Stellons, well, that person had best change their mind. Looking at Othello, one couldn't be sure if she was part wolf, part Shepherd, or just part of what she was. And she could bark, and she could howl—just ask the neighbors.

Othello loved kids, and they loved her. She especially liked girls because they always said pretty words to her, and she would drop and roll over so they could rub her tummy. But she did not like men, no way—especially men who had beards and wore baseball caps. Othello was a trained guard dog and was suspicious of any man whose eyes were not visible. It was part training and breeding-part Husky and part German shepherd.

"I got it, Mom. That Othello... Someday, she's gonna get hers," threatened Mickey as he plopped down at the kitchen table. His bacon and egg omelet—along with some toast—and strawberry jam-were awaiting him. He was famished and wasted no time in gobbling his breakfast. He gave half his toast to Othello and lifted Mort off the table before Mom caught him slurping milk from Mickey's bowl. Mort was a classic American tabby with cinnamon swirls on his sides, a waffle-patterned belly that swayed and brushed the floor, and a thick cane-like tail.

Mickey's mother, Jilly, was perfect. At least, Mickey thought so. They had been one for three years and they had come to do everything together and become best buddies. Still, she often spoke of Mickey's father, Reynolds. He had been chiseled from head to foot, and had loved farming, hunting and trapping. Mickey's mom never talked about what had happened to his father, though, so all Mickey knew was that his Dad had taught him how to hunt and fish. And *that now, he* was on his own.

But Mickey's dad had been shot—with his own pistol. He'd been found in his wrecked pickup; it had looked like he'd been in an accident. While nothing had ever come from the sheriff's investigation, it was thought that Reynolds' gun had accidentally discharged during the accident and killed him.

"Reynolds was so careful around guns," was all Mickey's mother would say. "*He grew* up around guns. He was in the Army. Something happened out there..."

And then, her voice would quiver and go quiet. Her blue eyes would moisten and close as if to hide what she was thinking from Mickey and nothing more would be said. Mickey also tried to keep his pain from his mom. After all, he was the man of the house.

"Mom, today is the day to sign up for the contest," he told her excitedly after swallowing a big bite of cereal. "And I'm going to win. I've been waiting for this since last year. You said I could enter," he added, seeking her assurance.

Before she could reply, Mickey blurted, "Me and Stu are going to team up. We got it all figured out. Just you watch us."

Jilly never said a word, but nodded approvingly, her warm smile competing with the sunshine outside the kitchen window. She knew how important this contest was to Mickey. When dad and son had hunted, Mickey had tossed and turned the whole eve of the adventure.

"I know. Your dad often said you were a chip off the old block," she mused under her breath. Mickey had the same mannerisms as his dad. He walked, talked, and gestured the same. Both would rather be outdoors than elsewhere. And their drive to be first in everything often got in the way of fair play; but, in the end, it was all fun.

Mickey picked at his omelet, carefully corralling the onions and green things on one side of his plate so they would not to touch the rest of the food. Othello lay next to his chair, awaiting her serving, even though she'd already had her first round of toast. Othello was not a picky eater, as was made obvious by her girth. Mickey's dad had always said that Othello was built for endurance, not speed.

As his mom finished clearing the dishes, Mickey pulled a goldenrod-colored flyer from his shirt pocket. He carefully unfolded it, being careful *not to tear it*. It was the only one he had, and it had to be turned in that day, and he knew that old Mr. Walser, the drug store owner, was a grump who liked things done in a certain way. He had often observed Mr. Walser sweeping the sidewalk in front of his store even when there wasn't any dirt to be swept. Mickey didn't want to get in his way, since grumpy was in charge of the Contest.

Mickey pressed the fall-colored flyer on the table just like he had seen his mom do when ironing clothes. Each stroke flattened more of the creases until it was just about perfect. He held the paper up and motioned for his mother to look.

"Check this over before I go, will ya?" he asked.

Jilly daintily took the flyer by the corner, as if to tease her son. She moved her lips while her eyes scanned downward.

"You do know that a lot of local hunters will be going after this. There will probably be a number of folks from all around the state wanting it as well," she said.

"Yup," he replied in a strong, confident voice.

Jilly read it aloud as if she were a carnival worker trying to entice someone into playing a game of chance. She had read the announcement to Mickey many times in recent weeks, but Mickey pretended each time that it was the very first time he'd heard it.

WALSER DRUG STORE & HARDWARE
PROUDLY ANNOUNCES ITS 12TH ANNUAL

THE LONGEST FEATHER CONTEST

SEPTEMBER 12[11] THRU SEPTEMBER 18TH

Any registered participant who brings in the
longest natural pheasant feather by 5:00 p.m.
on Sunday, September 18th,
will win a brand-new, in-the-box

REMINGTON DOUBLE BARREL
***12-GAUGE SHOTGUN* ($200 value!!!)**

The feather must be naturally grown and will be

measured from the tip of the quill to the end of the feather.

Completed official form must be received by Walser Drug Store & Hardware on or before September 18th. Clark County Sheriffs Department will measure and record all entries.

Name	Date

Walser Drug Store & Hardware	Date

On his way to and from school, Mickey had purposely walked by Walser's so he could stare at *his* shotgun one more time. He could already *see his name* and *his* fingerprints on it. On frosty mornings, he would draw targets on the windowpane in his bedroom and see himself and Othello trudging through cornfields, just daring a pheasant to challenge them. *BOOM! One less* dumb bird! He could smell the powder and feel the recoil rock against his shoulder. It hurt, but *it* was a good hurt.

"I gotta go. Stu's waitin' and you how Stu is 'bout waitin'," he told his mom as he tacked the flyer back into his shirt pocket, pulled his hooded sweatshirt over his head and flung the front door open.

2

Mickey stood on the edge of the steps and peered across the street. He made his breath puff out of his mouth like great plumes of smoke from a locomotive. It helped him adjust to the frosty crystals in the air. He shivered and pulled the drawstrings on his hood a little tighter.

Stu was up to his usual antics. He just finished drawing the last of his stickmen on a car's frosted windows and pulled his hands inside the sleeves of his sweatshirt. He abruptly stopped in the middle of the street, came to attention, and saluted Mickey in his usual impish manner

"Stu, let's go. We have places to go, people to see, and things to do". he boasted.

He jumped over the railing and landed in a pile of crisp leaves, almost disappearing from sight. *Cold country is coming—-that's for sure,* he thought. The brownish-red leaves splashed aside under his trudging *footsteps.*

Stu caught up to Mickey and tried to trip him from behind

by stepping on Mickey's heel. Mickey stumbled, but caught himself and pushed back at Stu. They were the best of friends. Stu lived with his grandfather, but spent most of his time at Mickey's house. Stu's parents were killed in a car accident shortly after his birth, and Jilly practically adopted him.

"Got your registration done?" he asked Stu.

"Yup, here it is. See?" responded Stu as he thrust his wrinkled parchment in Mickey's face. Stu's straight, jet-black hair jutted from underneath his cap. His eyes had a natural squint to them. His classmates teased him about his evil, beady eyes, crossing their arms in front of their faces or forming crosses with their two index fingers.

"Good." Mickey grinned as he slapped Stu on the back.

The two of them walked together, step for step. Each made sure they did not step on any cracks in the sidewalk because they'd been told that something bad could happen to their mothers if they did step on one. They squatted like coiled springs and leaped across each fracture in the cement, often pretending it was a huge gully. They laughed and taunted each other by grabbing at each other's sleeves, trying to see who would falter first. Othello, running alongside them, couldn't have eared less about their game.

"Race ya to the corner," Stu yelled as he sprinted ahead of Mickey. Stu had always been the faster of the two. His quickness helped him avoid hallway confrontations with fellow students.

"No fair," Mickey hollered as Stu quickly sprinted ahead of him, Othello nipping at his hands. Othello always loved a good race and rarely lost—though more often than not, Stu could match her.

As they approached the comer, a black pickup roared to the intersection. The truck slid to a stop and the driver's window lowered, but only an inch or two. The driver appeared to be nothing but a ball of hair sitting behind the steering wheel. But, as if by magic, the whiskers parted and words came out. The boys saw two white orbs with black dots in their centers staring at them, almost burning through them. But where was his nose?

"Where ya boys goin' in such a hurry?" the driver demanded.

Startled by the commotion but unafraid, Stu bragged, "Ahhhhh! Walser's'. We're gonna win. Ain't no doubt 'bout it."

"Do you want a ride?" yelled the hairy head. "Hop in. Plenty of room. We're headed that way too."

The passenger door flung open and an arm waved for them to get in. The boys could see a gun rack in the rear window with two cradled rifles. The passenger alit and approached them. He was small in height, but his bulging biceps left no room in his sleeves.

"Come, on boys," he cracked. "Even got room for yer dog."

No time to look for oncoming cars! Mickey thought. He had heard stories of what happened to kids in big cities who took rides with strangers-the only things found after the fact were their *shoes, if* that.

Othello taunted the truck driver and his passenger with her barks and gyrations. Her teeth glistened and steam seemed to come from her mouth. Her ears laid back and she positioned herself between the boys and the truck. "Othello, come," demanded her master.

And then suddenly, Mickey and Stu ran as if their lives depended on it-like the cracks in the sidewalk weren't *there*. Stu and Othello led the way; Mickey had never run that fast before but he was closing in on them. His heart was in his throat and the air's ice crystals burned his lungs.

Mickey faintly heard the screeching of tires but didn't stop to see which way the truck headed. He, Stu and Othello just flat-out ran toward the front doors of their safe haven, Walser's Drug Store and Hardware. Once they reached their destination, they stopped and put their hands on their knees, gasping for breath. They laughed, but they figured that they had escaped a fate worst than death.

3

As the boys entered the drug store, a puff of smoke curled around the door and leaped at them as if trying to capture them. The blast of heat from the pot-belly stove was almost as bad. And the laughter from the grandpas hit a high level pitch which was an indication that one of them must have told a whopper of a story.

"Whew! My eyes are burning!" cried Stu.

"Mine too," moaned Mickey. "And I'm still *wheezing from* running from the fur-head." He laughed.

But they entered the store anyway, with their registration forms in their hands, and looked for the area where they could submit them. Even the jars filled with peppermint sticks, sugar cookies, *taffy* and penny candies did not lure them from their mission, and the comic books rack didn't entice them either.

As was customary on Saturday morning, the town's grandpas were hanging around the store, sharing stories and laughing as they soaked up heat from the stove. Mickey remembered that his dad had on stopped to talk with them when he and Mickey had come into the store together.

Stu *tugged on* Mickey's arm and nodded toward a rather slight figure behind the counter—Mrs. Walser, She was a friendly lady but she rarely spoke, though it was more due to her heritage than her manners. Shiloh-that was her first name-was a Native American tribe member and very proud of her ancestry, which could be traced back to Sacagawea and Charbonneau. She and her husband had met in college, where she'd been studying Native American history and he'd been pursuing his degree in pharmacy. Now, she was the mother of Breathe, a Classmate of Mickey's. The schoolyard joke was that Breathe was the result of a raid on Mrs. Walser's village by hunters and trappers, but nothing could have been further from the truth. Breathe had been a college baby; she'd been christened Breathtaking Blue Sky, which had been shortened to Breathe. "What do you boys want now?" the Mrs. Walser inquired.

Both boys thrust their wrinkled, brown papers onto the counter and smiled at each other. "Here are our registrations for the contest. We're gonna win the shotgun," boasted Stu. "Might as well take it down and put my name on it," Mickey added.

"OK, boys. All seems to be in order. Anything else on your minds?" groused the old crab—that was what the kids called her when she wasn't around.

"Nope," the two answered in unison.

Then, both Mickey and Stu were drawn to the table where the prize was displayed. They seemed to be hypnotized by the glare on its long, shiny, blue barrel. The last time the two had stood in one place for so long was when the circus had been in town and the sword swallower had eaten a sword and belched fire. Stu often talked about running away from home to join the circus just to learn how to do that, and once in a while tried to do it, but he never got to the end of town before it was suppertime and he had to go home.

"Mickey," said a voice behind them the voice of an angel. "What are doing today and can I go with you guys? Please?" She put her hands on her hips and blew a deep sigh that parted her locks and revealed her moist baby blues. She smiled-an irksome smile, painful but pleasing. She had eyes that burned right through anybody who refused her demands.

"Well!" she went on. "Are ya gonna answer me or do I have to arm wrestle you down again?"

It was a voice that the boys knew immediately, though they didn't dare look at her. After all, she was *a girl,* and girls had germs! Mickey and Stu both gulped and practically fell over each other.

"Hi, Breathe." Mickey responded with a smile. "We ain't got nuthin' planned. Just dropped off our registration for the contest." He thrust his hands deep into his Wrangler pockets and looked painfully at his boots. He could feel heat rising on his neck and was sure that Stu and the old folks could see it as well.

"I got mine in, too. Just in case," Breathe teased.

"Let's go, Stu," Mickey ordered. As they headed toward the door, the laughter got louder and louder. Mickey was sweating now and it wasn't from the pot-bellied stove. Even Stu had to smirk—but that was the least of his worries. What about Breathe? Had she seen his discomfort?

Suddenly, he felt a thud on his chest, but his eyes couldn't focus. They were trying to, but and all he could see was fur! He had run right into the fur-ball from earlier, the hairy head from the pickup, who was as wide as he was tall.

"'Scuse me," Mickey offered as he stumbled to regain his footing. The fur-ball had him in his grasp. Mickey tore away and ran outside, half embarrassed and half scared. Stu followed and so did Breathe.

"Wait for me. Wait up. I got somethin' to tell you!" she called, her reddish hair streaming behind her as she raced after the boys.

"Darn ya," Mickey threatened the whiskered man. "Watch where your goin'. I ought to kick your butt. Next time, I'll..." He spun around with a clenched fist, but realized that the group around the stove was watching him. The room went silence as the bearded man walked toward the table where the prize was displayed.

"Mighty fine shotgun if I do say so myself," he said. "No need for you boys to get excited. It'll look good in my truck's gun rack. I'll be back to pick it up." He spoke in a threatening tone and never blinked. Only the sounds of creaking floor boards disturbed the muteness of the moment as the man sauntered toward the door.

"You pardners have a nice day now," he mused, as he slammed the door after him. The old gents mumbled among themselves, one of them creeping toward the window in a hunched over posture as if to avoid detection.

The black truck scorched the pavement with two distinct trails as it spun its oversized tires, competing with the radio inside the store that was blaring a country twang.

4

I hate to think of winter, Mickey thought, closing the porch door behind him, glad to be back home. His dad had always said that there were two seasons in a year: road repair and winter. Mickey didn't know about all that stuff, but he knew about blowing snow and icy winds. Just thinking about them sent shivers down his back. He closed the top button on his jacket and flipped up the collar as if to block the chill.

Sure wish I had a coat like Othello's, he mused as he walked to the kitchen, in search of his mom. *Great in winter though not so great in summer!*

Reynolds had been a good dad. He'd often taken his son with him when he'd traveled throughout his district. He'd had a triangular territory that stretched from Eagle Butte to Raven's Hollow to Echo Valley. Mickey had always wanted to be like his dad; he wanted to be a biologist and work for the state game and fish division. He loved the wide-open *outdoors and* all *forms of wildlife, great* and small, but most of all, he loved to ride in the pickup, listen to his dad tell stories, and eat! There was nothing better than cutting a chunk of ring bologna with his hunting knife and slapping it on bun smothered in mustard. *Mmmmmm...good!* He could almost taste its sting.

It had never been determined how Reynolds had died. After law enforcement had finished its investigation, the report stated that is had been a one—vehicle rollover most likely caused by inattentive driving.

"Mom," Mickey asked, finding her washing dishes in the sink. "How did Dad die, anyways?"

Jilly felt an all—too—familiar numbness creep over her body. It crawled along her edges and momentarily paralyzed her. She could not lift her hands to her hips, like she usually did when she needed a moment to collect her thoughts. She just stared aimlessly *out* the kitchen window. She had known that Mickey would ask her that question someday, and had known that she would have to answer him. And today was that day.

Jilly wanted to run, but she was frozen. Courageously, she forced herself to turn. It seemed to take forever. Her blushing cheeks warmed her composure, prying loose the invisible grip that seemed to choke her. She took a deep breath, exhaled slowly, and brushed imaginary crumbs from her apron.

"Well, they weren't sure," she began, looking down at her son. "They said he probably fell asleep and headed for the ditch. *The* marks suggested that he overcorrected the steering to get back on the road, and the truck rolled several times...There was an unexplainable streak of black paint particle embedded in its compressed, left-rear fender... He died before help arrived. An anonymous telephone call to the sheriff's office alerted police to the accident." She stopped, and then added quickly, "The caller has never been identified."

What she didn't say was that all leads in the case had fallen dormant as the calls had lessened. Although the case was still not officially closed, other issues in the sheriff's office had pushed the investigation onto the "to do" pile.

She also didn't tell him about the caller's lisp and raspy voice. Not too many townsfolk know about it as well. Nor did she tell him about the rumors of strangers in the area where Reynolds had died.

She reached down and hugged Mickey as if to squeeze the life out of him. He reached up and put his gangly arms around her neck.

"It's ok, Mom. We'll be ok," he whispered. He spoke with a certainty that made Jilly feel as if Reynolds had never left. Mickey was so much like his dad. His voice, his confidence and his physical strength cloaked her in a sense of security, even if only for the moment. She clung to that feeling; it brought back so many memories.

"Stu and I are going down to Echo Valley to hunt for pheasants," Mickey told her as he heard Stu climbing the front porch steps. "We have to find the one with the longest feather. You know, Mom, and then I can win that new shotgun. Oh, I guess Breathe is coming too."

Breathe preferred to be with the boys rather than to do things with the other girls in her class. Thinking about this made Mickey smile.

"Mickey, let's go!" came the cry from the porch. "We got lots to do and a long way to go. Daylight is burning!" Stu always tried to copy John Wayne's lines from the movies, but he never got them correct.

"Mom, can Othello go with us?" Mickey asked, pulling away from her. "She'll be a good protector, and she needs the workout."

Jilly was hesitant, but she knew how much Othello loved to walk. All anyone had to do was say "truck" or "walk" and Othello was at the front door, wagging her tail aimlessly.

"Just be home before dark," she said, nodding her head at Mickey, "and you be careful in Echo Valley! Tomorrow is church. Remember, there are some strange happenings going on there. You hear me?" she pleaded, but her fears fell on deaf ears. She knew of those dangers from conversations she'd had with Reynolds. Echo Valley had been a part of his territory and if anybody knew of strange proceedings, it was Reynolds.

The door opened and Othello pounced on Breathe. They seemed to have a special bond.

"Othello," the children's voices called in unison. Othello bounded down the steps as if she knew where they were going.

Echo Valley had been a silver-mining town at the turn of the century. There had been talk lately of reopening the mine, as drilling methods had improved, but there were varied forces working against it, including reports that the mine and surrounding valley were haunted by specters of men who had once worked the mines. There were stories of Chinese ghosts walking from the cemetery to the mine entrance in the early morning and back under the cloak of darkness. Even when the town had been robust and the mine productive, no one ever had seen the workers who had provided most of the services. There seemed to be a shadow town below the real town itself, replete with streets, stores, businesses and residences. The whole area was unsafe due to cave-ins of the many tunnels that traversed under the streets.

Stu had a special kinship with the old silver mine. His gramps told many family stories that traced his heritage back to the formative days of the mining community. His family tree, according to Gramps, suggested that they had worked many jobs during the community's heyday. They'd been miners, gardeners, storekeepers and blacksmiths.

Why, there hadn't been a job they didn't do. Stu was always entertained by his gramps' storytelling, especially where fiction overtook fact. He knew that it did, but enjoyed the stories nevertheless.

But of more interest to Stu, Mickey and Breathe was that Echo Valley was the state's foremost breeding ground for Chinese pheasants. The pheasants had been brought over from China by the immigrants who had come, willingly or unwillingly, to work the mines and do other common labor. The pheasants were strong birds known for their cunning and trickery. They could run, duck and hide in the underbrush and then reappear far down the field from their stalkers. And, these birds were special because they sported the longest tail feathers of any game bird in the area.

"Are we going to walk through the cemetery at night?" asked Breathe. She had more courage than most of the boys in her class. "Let's see how deep we can go in the cave. I brought a flashlight.

Maybe we can climb down into the underground passageways and look for old bones. Who knows? We might find bags of silver hidden by the miners. Then we could buy shotguns for all of us." The words seemed never to reach Mickey's and Stu's ears. They smiled, but did not respond. They had heard this all too many times. They mumbled to each other that perhaps that was how she'd gotten her name—she never seemed to breathe! They teased her often that her nickname should be "Blue Sky," for she on talked as long as the sky was tall. When she started on some topic, the boys would point to the sky and laugh, and accuse her of being more like her pa than her ma. This did nothing but infuriate her.

"We'll see," chimed the boys. That seemed to satisfy her—for the moment, anyway.

Breathe picked up a stick and hurled it in front of Othello, who raced to catch it in the air, but caught it on the bounce and brought it back to her. Othello walked alongside Breathe, awaiting a treat, but a pat on the head had to do for the time being.

They stopped along the rim top and shared some cookies and Kool-Aid that Ally had prepared. The snack hit the spot, as they had walked nearly seven miles from the highway. Othello got her share as well.

They sat on a large boulder along the road's edge. Each raised their hand above their eyes to shield the sun's glare. For a moment, it was as if they had taken a step back in time and were all Native .Americans, watching over sacred ground. The valley held special meaning for each of them for personal reasons— family, generations, ancestry. Only the gusts of wind interrupted their solitude at the crossroads of where and when.

5

They packed up and descended the winding road into Echo Valley. They observed tire tracks leading the way, but the heavy ground fog prevented them from seeing much farther than ten feet in front of their noses. The dampness created a chilling effect, pushing the three of them closer together. They watched the frost come from their mouths and laughed at the steamy figures they tried to create.

Small ice droplets clung to the shrubs, and the wind cautioned them. There was an old smell about the valley that many old-timers attributed to the exploiting of the land. Native Americans claimed it was the gods seeking revenge for the violation of the sacredness of the mountains. Others said it was the Oriental ghosts of the past demanding payment for the blood, sweat and tears of their sons and daughters.

"Look out for the snake, Breathe," shouted Stu. Breathe screeched and then pushed Stu. The boys laughed and slapped each other's hands in a victory celebration.

"Not funny. I'll get even with both of you!" she yelled. They all laughed and Othello barked as if she'd enjoyed the prank.

The tall reeds and tumbleweeds alongside the road swayed with the varying wind currents. Their whistling chorus created a cautioning alert to the children, but none paid much attention. Mickey snapped off a long reed and used it to tickle Breathe's ear. She sprang into a jog ahead of the boys, tauntingly looking back. Only Othello pranced beside her. The boys raced to catch her, but she sprinted ahead with ease.

As they reached the bottom of the valley, Othello stopped abruptly. Her ears perked up and she let out a low growl. Mickey quieted her with a gentle rubbing of her ears. They stood at the edge of to, peering down the first side street.

"If there are any ghosts, we'll be ready," threatened Mickey, great protector. After all, he was accustomed to ensuring his mother's safety and he felt he could provide security out here as well.

Mickey took a shotgun shell from a loop on his hunting vest, cracked open his gun's double barrel and loaded the shell into the right chamber; then, he repeated the step and snapped the two halves closed.

'Nothin' like being ready," he said, smirking. "You two be on the lookout. The pheasants are smart. They didn't live this long by standin' out in the open." The other two had heard this many times before, as they had hunted with him on numerous occasions. They mimicked his words, aped his gestures, and laughed quietly.

"Mickey, you are too serious," said Stu. "You need to lighten up. You're too much like your dad." Breathe nodded as well. Mickey cocked both hammers.

They sauntered down Main Street, or what was left of it. The once-proud town had deteriorated into piles of wood and glass and mounds of garbage. The *street was* rutted and pocked with potholes. Teenagers had held drinking parties there, as evidenced by charred boards that had been pillaged *from* the buildings and burned in the center of the street.

The windows on the buildings had long ago lost their glass,

and tattered remnants of curtains hung limply through the casements. Doors had been demolished and off-road four-wheelers had had their say on the insides of the structures where commerce had once flourished, families had shared bread, and the gospel had been read.

Mickey's eyes moved from left to right and back again as he looked for the slightest movement under a board or shrub. He tried to control his breathing as he had been taught, but his lungs puffed and he could feel his heart push outward. A cottontail streaked from under the clapboard porch, raced across the pockmarked street and found refuge under a pile of sticks. Mickey relaxed his trigger finger and eased both hammers.

"*Whew,*" *he* sighed. "Too bad it wasn't one of those pheasants. They way it thrashed, it would have been big enough to sport a winner."

Breathe and Stu also caught their breath. They had frozen in their tracks when Mickey had lifted the double-barrel.

The trio moved stealthily down the main street, looking for any sign of bird tracks. Othello was more interested in what he could arouse from under a turned-over wash tub.

"Keep your eyes peeled for any tracks," Mickey instructed them. "You know these birds are smart, and they can run faster than they fly. You almost have to step on one to get them up." The two students again aped their instructor's mannerisms. Mickey knew what they were doing, but chose to ignore them as he had become accustomed to their antics. He was the experienced leader, not them. Someday, they would realize it and listen to him.

6

The frost was rapidly disappearing as the golden rays of sun began burning their signature on the landscape. Droplets fell from all angles of the wooden structures, escaping the invaders. Steam lifted heavenward as if an iron had pressed the rooftops, and the fog gave way to brownish-black buildings. Cricket chirps were replaced by the barn swallow's warning shrill. A taunting gust swept down the street to awaken another day's life for whomever cared.

"Aughhhhhh!" cried Mickey as he sprawled face-down on the greasy dirt street. The shotgun did a cartwheel in the air and landed ten feet in front of him. His backpack was covering his he, and he rolled sideways. From the loud snap, he knew instantly that he had hurt his ankle. The pain rocketed up his leg. He reached for his throbbing ankle, but the pothole he had tripped on prevented him from reaching down to hold it.

Breathe and Stu grabbed him by his shoulder and pulled him out of the hole, then dragged him to a dry section of the street. Othello barked in excitement and nuzzled Mickey with her nose.

"Stupid me," Mickey said. "I should have known that there were holes all over this darn street. How many times have we been here before? Get me up!" The other two struggled, but lifted him by providing support under his arms.

He hobbled to where his shotgun had landed. The barrels lay facing the stock. It had broken in half. *Mickey* stared *in* disbelief. He picked up the two pieces. It was the only shotgun he owned, and it had been given to him by his dad. It was just an ordinary shotgun. Now what was he going to do? How was he going to shoot a pheasant, let alone one with the longest feather, and how was he going to win that *new* shotgun? He really needed a new shotgun now. A thousand questions raced through his mind.

"Should we go home?" asked Breathe. She looked at Mickey's swollen ankle and knew it would take a lot longer to get home than it had to get there. Stu had equal concerns but knew that Mickey was stubborn and did like to be told anything, especially what to do.

"No," Mickey retorted. "Maybe I can find wire or something to bind the two pieces together, and it will still shoot."

"No, Mick. I'm talking about your ankle," said Breathe. She took the scarf from around her neck and wove a figure-eight with it around his ankle.

Now try that," she demanded.

The three of them looked like something out of the American Revolution as they moved in solidarity down the street. All they needed was the American flag, drums and a piccolo. Breathe and Stu cradled Mickey under each of his arms, and Mickey cradled the broken keepsake. Othello was in her own world as she chased a piece of paper floating capriciously about on the wind current.

As they turned right and headed toward the cemetery, they heard what they thought were voices.

"What's that?" asked Stu. "Nothin'," replied Breathe.

"It's just your imagination playing tricks on you," said Mickey. "Just like the time we were pushing over outhouses on Halloween and you thought you heard something and took off running, only to run the wrong way and fall in the open outhouse hole." He laughed.

The subsequent events of that swim replayed in their minds, and they laughed nervously. Othello barked; Stu reached down to comfort her and grabbed her collar. The nervous laughs turned silent and their hearts climbed into their throats. Was the story of the Chinese ghosts...real?

They quickly moved hide themselves. Mickey's pain was gone—for the moment, anyway. They moved alongside the wall of the old saloon. They peered through the building's gaping boards but saw only shards of broken glass and remnants of chairs and tables. A shutter on a window creaked in the wind and a strip of wallpaper danced in unison with its counterpart across the hallway.

"What was that?" exclaimed Breathe. A shrapnel of tarpaper brushed against her head. She ducked and cowered as it swung back again.

They reached the corner of the building, but saw nothing. They moved cautiously across the alley to a large cottonwood tree. It had long since served its original purpose and now; it awaited its demise as firewood or in the longer term petrified wood. Stu had heard stories about the "hanging tree" and how its leaves turned red in the fall because the blood of its victims flowed from its roots to the heavens.

They squatted to plot their next move. Othello was panting, and she lay down at their feet. Mickey spotted a piece of bailing wire and asked Stu to retrieve it for him. He took out his broken weapon and splintered it together as close to its original shape as he could. He bound the two parts as tightly as he could using sticks on both sides as a splint, and then twisted the two ends of wire tightly around the stock with a sturdy, thick branch. He raised the gun to his shoulder and aimed down the barrel.

"Good as new," he whispered. He was more concerned with the shotgun's health than his own. Under the circumstance, they were all relieved, and it showed in their posture and the resultant high-fives.

7

"We need to head home. Our moms will be worried about us," lamented Breathe. "We should have left a couple of hours ago," Stu chimed in.

"It's getting dark and we need to find shelter from the cold and the wind," responded Mickey. "We're better off here than trying to walk home. My ankle will never hold up, and you two can't carry me. Plus, the throbbing is really beginning to hurt." He grimaced in pain.

"What are we goin' to do? We're going to freeze to death," Stu said, sounding afraid.

They huddled together to draw warmth from each other and stave off the chills. They had not come prepared to stay into the night and, what was more, all night *and* outdoors. Their hearts pounded within each of them as if to demand escape from the fear and the cold.

"We'll send Othello home and when they see we're not with her, they'll come lookin' for us," offered Mickey.

"Great idea," said Stu, chortling. "What was that?" begged Breathe.

Othello's heart was racing, and she panted louder. Her *ears were erect, her* stance *was* taut, and a low snarl spewed from her clenched teeth. Breathe calmed her with slow strokes down her brisket and wrapped her soft hands around Othello's mouth. Othello squirmed to free herself, but Breathe maintained the grip.

Othello's mannerisms suggested that something was stirring outside, but the children could not see beyond the high, picket fence surrounding the old dry goods and confectionary store.

"Othello! Go home, girl. Go home and bring back help. Go! Now!" ordered Mickey.

Othello leaped out of Breathe's clutch and sprinted down the moonlit pathway leading to the main street, and disappeared into the darkness.

"We love you, Othello," Breathe murmured softly. Othello and she had always had a special bond. The boys felt the same, but they dared not let each other—or Breathe—hear their sobs.

Boom! Boom! Two loud reports were heard. The trio stood frozen. One more shot echoed. Their hearts sank. They reached for each other, but said nothing.

Day crept into night so slowly, and the darkness seemed to make the cold penetrate even deeper. They moved inside the dilapidated building, which was more of a lean-to than a structure. There, they found refuge from the elements and pulled an old, straw mattress over them. It smelled musty, but it was warm. They took turns staying awake, but that was futile, as they all stayed awake, alert and scared.

"Let's hope," prayed Stu.

"We'll get through this," Mickey encouraged. "We've been in tight spots before." "Let's hope," echoed Breathe.

"We'll stay right here," Mickey went on. "The sun will be comin' up pretty soon and then we'll see better what's out there."

They tried to comfort each other, but, no one said what they really felt about having no food, no water and no coats. However, their looks betrayed their courage which was a false courage at best.

The voices grew louder and a scraping was heard along the outside wall of the store. The trio stooped down to avoid discovery. They could hear footsteps slosh through the muck alongside the building.

"This whole idea is *crazy*," complained one of the voices outside. "We should wait until winter. Then nobody is around here. The hunters are gone. The spelunkers are back in school and the want-to-be silver and gold panners have given up."

"What was that?" wondered Stu. "Shhhhhlh," whispered Breathe.

Mickey and Stu sat up and moved to the doorway leading to the backyard. They had heard *those* voices before. They peered around the doorjamb with Stu tucked under Mickey's right armpit. They surveyed the landscape and caught sight of two figures waddling through the mud. The moonlight cast enough light for them to see the outline of the men's bodies. One was big and thick throughout, and the other was slender and tall. Where had Mickey and Stu seen them before?

"Aren't those the two—" began Stu, but he was interrupted by Mickey's well-placed elbow.

"Shhhh," said Mickey. "I think so."

The backyard was littered with old tires and what appeared to be piles of garbage. An old car body disrupted the boys' line of sight, and the two figures disappeared.

"Everybody ok?" asked Mickey. He could faintly see Stu's and Breathe's huddled shadows against the dimly moonlit wallpaper.

"Yup, but I'm getting 'cold just sitting here," responded Stu in a shivering voice. "Me, too," chorused Breathe.

It had been a long night already, but it wasn't over yet. Sunrise was several hours away. The three snuggled together, to become one and stave off the shivers. They jockeyed for the warmest position against the warmest body. Regardless of their efforts to stay awake, sleep paralyzed them and they blended with the night.

8

Canary-yellow light broke gently through the barren limbs of the black cottonwood, whose limbs seemed to awaken with upward stretching. The sun's rays chased around the charred chimneys of the abandoned, warped, wooden hulks, an occasional, golden glint bouncing off the tin strips that once proudly masked missing tarpaper and shingles. A single, birdlike outline perched atop a power pole in the awakening sky, revealing its red breast as it was joined by several kindred spirits seeking to greet the new morning. Steam rose from the rustic rooftops as the sun chased down the darkness.

Warm wisps sun patted the children's faces and awakened them. They had survived under nighttime's cloak.

"How's your ankle?" asked Stu.

"Very sore and swollen," Mickey responded. "I don't dare take my shoe off or I'll never get it back on."

The two rose and helped Mickey to his feet. He used the damaged shotgun as a crutch and hobbled to the back doorway.

They all peered out the opening and saw two pheasant roosters and three hens eating gravel from a sand pile. No sooner were they seen than they flew low to some buck brush and vanished.

"Just my luck," said Mickey with a chuckle. "My dad said they always run faster to cover than they fly."

"Yup," agreed Stu. "And if you didn't have back luck, you wouldn't have any luck at all!"

They all laughed and exchanged knuckle handshakes. It was their morning communion. They ate the remainder of their snacks and savored each bite as if it were their last.

The trio then walked slowly through the backyard, toward the rickety fence that separated them from the drainage ditch. They looked through the slits in the fence and ducked down. There was that black truck the boys had seen in town a couple days before! Stu peeked through a hole in the fence for a second look, and a slice of silver caught his eye. It nearly blinded him and for a second, he struggled to *refocus. But he* knew what he was seeing—it was that truck that had slowly followed him and Mickey as they'd walked to Mickey's home after registering for the longest feather contest. The driver had asked them if they'd wanted a ride home.

The flaxen reeds partially hid the vehicle from view, but there was no mistake. It was the truck. Stu's and Mickey's hearts sank once again and they looked at each other with fear in their eyes.

"What if they saw us?" asked Breathe.

"I don't think they did. I didn't see anybody around. Did you?" asked Stu.

They all shook their heads in agreement and again surveyed the landscape. The sun was directly in their eyes and they squinted to differentiate moving from nonmoving objects.

"I'm going to get a closer look at what's goin' on over there," charged Breathe.

Before the boys could react, she crawled on her stomach to an opening in the fence. Mickey was unable to grab her legs as she scrambled through the opening, and Stu was preoccupied with watching the field for any suspicious *movement.*

She crawled down the embankment and into the creek bed.

She was soon bathed in deep, brown mud and green, slimy gunk. It covered her face and all the way down the front of her body. It didn't take long for her to look like she lived in the muddy bog. Breathe rolled over to push up the barbed wire and scoot under it without getting caught. Now, she was really baptized. From top to bottom and from back to front, there wasn't a bit of clothing or exposed skin. She swallowed mud and muck and wiped algae from her eyes. The boys could not tell the difference between her and the contour of the creek bed.

And that was what they liked about Breathe—and what scared them about her. She was all boy, even a Reynolds-type boy! Sometimes, she was more boy than was good for her. She knew no fear; she *caused fear!*

Suddenly, Mickey saw the golden reeds sway. He nudged Stu and pointed in the general direction of the movement. Stu nodded. There was a brownish thing—Breathe—slithering slowly up the other embankment. Stu almost broke out in laughter, but Mickey put his finger to his lips, signaling him to remain quiet. Both boys smiled and buried their faces in the earth.

And then, they heard the voices.

"Let's get this stuff loaded before somebody comes," groused the bearded man, approaching the truck the boys had seen.

"Yeah, we're pushin' our luck," replied his slender companion.

The first man was easily over six feet tall. His hips were several inches above the pickup's tailgate. His torso was chiseled in a V shape and his biceps looked like two sides of ham hocks. He wore one of those t-shirts that didn't have sleeves—or, the sleeves had been ripped out. His locks flowed from underneath his sweat-stained, red baseball cap, which was pulled low over his forehead. He had no difficulty lifting his share of the load. His beard covered his entire face, including his mouth.

His sidekick was tall and rather thin in stature. His shirt draped over him, disguising any body definition. He was constantly pulling up his Levi's, as he had no hips on which to anchor his belt. His bald head was sunburned and his face was pocked with acne scars. He met his match with each gunny sack he lifted into the truck, as they appeared to weigh more than him.

The men continued to load several tan gunny sacks in the back of the pickup. Each bag was heavy and awkward, and it took both men to hoist each sack into the truck bed. The stout man railed on the slighter man.

"Why do they always send a boy to do a man's job? You should give me half of your pay for doing your work," yelled the bigger man.

There was no reply. The lighter man was more concerned with any intruders than he was with the task of loading the contraband. He must have had the eyes of an eagle, as he detected movement in the grass.

Over there," he hollered to the furry-faced one.

"What now? Are you seeing things again? If the wind blows, you see the boogie man. Get back to work so we can get out of here and deliver the goods," chided the taller man.

"I thought 1 saw something move in the grass over there. I'm sure of it," said the other one.

Breathe froze. She could hear the two talking and feared she had been discovered. They continue to talk about ghost, goblins and seeing things. She raised her head, but saw nothing. She turned over and looked back, but saw nothing. She turned back and lay quietly, trying to become one with the earth and sky.

The truck doors opened and slammed shut. With the start of the engine, the truck lurched forward and labored it way across the open area, toward the gravel road. The pickup bed was covered with a light-blue tarp anchored at each corner to ensure the privacy of the cargo. Its load pushed the truck's frame down on its shocks and somewhat flattened the tires; nevertheless, the transport reached the edge and lumbered up the incline to the road's surface.

Breathe rolled over and looked about. Seeing nothing, she rose to one knee and scouted the area once more. She crouched and began moving toward the fence, where the boys were secluded. Her tennis shoes were caked with mud, as was her entire torso. She tried to run, but a waddle was the best she could do.

She looked over bath shoulders to see if anyone was following her. As she turned forward, her chin smacked into the chest of the tall man. She fell into a heap of mud, straw and leaves. She didn't move or groan. She was lifeless.

Mickey and Stu were stunned. The tall man bent over and placed his hands on his knees and looked at Breathe. He stood erect and looked in the direction she'd been running. He stared for the longest time and then began walking toward them.

"*Let's go,* Jake. We got a schedule to meet," the stout man hollered after him.

Jake stopped, raised his right hand, then pointed and shook his index finger in the general direction of the boys, as if he knew they were there. He smirked.

"Johnny," he called, "help me get her up. She's breathing, but out stone cold."

Johnny and the other man came over and put one of Breathe's arms around his neck while Jake held her at the waist. Together, they carried her to the truck with her feet dragging and her head slouched downward.

Mickey and Stu watched intently. That was all they could do. This was not supposed to happen to one whose instincts were born of the wild.

9

Jilly's head lifted from her book. It was that familiar scratching she had heard so often. "Othello, is that you?" she asked. She laid the book face-down and rose from the couch. "I'm comin', girl."

She opened the door and Othello raced into the house, around the kitchen table and chairs and back around her. Her tail wig-wagged. She was panting and wild-eyed.

"What's the matter?" Jilly asked repeatedly. "Where are the kids? Where's Mickey? Are they all right?" She reached out and patted the dog's head.

Othello barked and headed to the door as if to beckon Jilly. She jumped and barked again.

"What is it?" Jilly asked. Othello jumped up and scratched at the front door. Her whining seemed to beg for Jilly's obedience.

A cold chill raced through Jilly. Her instincts never betrayed her, and the last time she'd had this feeling was when Reynolds had not come home at his usual time. The fist that had knocked on the door had been attached to Sheriff Barnes. Now, she wrestled again with the chill. Mothers are never wrong about those feelings when it comes to family, but Jilly didn't have time to dwell.

"Easy, Othello, I hear you. I need to call Barney. He'll know what to do." Jilly picked up the phone and dialed BL5-7874.

"Sheriff's Department. This is Deputy Luger. How may I help you?" The female voice was new to her. She had not talked to anyone at the department for a long time. The deputy spoke again, and Jilly cleared her throat.

"Is Barney, er, Sheriff Barnes in?"

"One moment please." *Click.*

"Sheriff Barnes." He hardly got his last name spoken before Jilly walked on his voice.

"Barney! Something's wrong!" she shouted. "They went to the old silver mine and only Othello Came back." Her words stumbled to get out through her tight throat.

"Jill. Just take a deep breath," the man's voice intoned. "Slow down and start at the beginning."

Jilly sat on a kitchen chair, inhaled deeply, and pulled Othello close to her, then explained the events that had led up to their current conversation.

Sheriff Barnes knew from previous experience that he had to move rapidly. The lives of three young citizens were in peril and he did want to make another unwelcomed visit to their parents.

"Jilly, we need to move fast," he advised. "You call Stu's Mom and Breathe's parents. I'll call the fire department and my deputies to form a search party. We'll meet at city hall in one hour."

No sooner had the two finished their talk than a loud knock interrupted Jilly's thoughts. Othello barked and headed to the door. Jilly followed and then cautiously cracked open the door, just enough to see who was there.

"Jilly, it's me, Sarah Chin, Stu's mom," the faceless voice offered. "Oh, Sarah, come in. I didn't recognize you," Jilly responded.

Sarah and Jilly sat at the kitchen table, with Othello in her normal, protective position at Jilly's feet. Sarah and Jilly were old high school classmates and their families had a long history together in Clark County. The two women had more similarities than differences—most notably that they had both lost their husbands through unusually strange circumstances.

Sarah's husband had been a high school history teacher who had enjoyed researching old towns. He had been fascinated with Echo Valley. In his spare time, he had driven to the old, silver-mining town and dug for artifacts. His body had been found in a sinkhole that had exposed the town's historical underground caves.

Evidently the cave-in had been caused by his weight. Although there were suspicions surrounding his death, it had been labeled an accident. As a result, archeological explorations required prior approval from the state. Essentially, the town was closed off from any future underground explorations.

Jilly explained the events of the day—that the three children had planned to hike to Echo Valley in search of pheasants and the hope of bringing home the longest feather to win the prized shotgun. But only Othello had returned. Then, she picked up the phone and dialed.

"Shiloh, this is Jilly," she said. "Is Breathe home? Is Mickey or Stu there?"

"No," came the reply. "I told you that Mickey is not welcome here, and I told Breathe that she is not to have anything to do with your boy. I told you that as well."

"Shiloh," Jilly said, "we need to put our differences aside for the moment. The kids, including Breathe, are nowhere to be found."

Shiloh was a friend of both of Jilly and Sarah. However, Shiloh's and Jilly's friendship had been broken when both of them had harbored a love interest in Reynolds. Reynolds had been the star athlete in their high school and had easily been the catch of the class. Jilly had won out and eventually, after Reynolds had returned from college, they'd gotten married. Shiloh had never forgotten, nor ever forgiven her, even though she'd done alright for herself. She had married the town pharmacist and was never in want of anything except Reynolds—a subtlety she never let Jilly, or anyone else, forget. Otherwise, she had the best of everything.

"Sheriff Barnes is forming a search party," Jilly went on, lecturing Shiloh as no one had ever dared to before, "and we are meeting in one hour at city hall. If you have any decency, you will put this pettiness of yours aside and help find our kids."

The spitfire, high school cheerleader had come out once again. Jilly slammed the phone down and looked at Sarah, who smiled faintly and wrung her hands nervously.

10

"Alright, listen up," Sheriff Barnes, Barney, demanded as he spoke to an assembly of about eleven townspeople and Othello. "I am deputizing you all to assist my office in searching for and finding Mickey, Stuart and Breathe. I want to emphasize that we will find them safe and return them to their families. The way I figure it, they just got lost and are waiting for us. So, let's head out to Echo Valley together. When we get to the big bend overseeing the valley, we'll assign who will be doing what. Are there any questions?"

"Are you going to issue any sidearms?" inquired Curly, the grocer.

"No way," responded the barber. "The last time you handled a pistol, you pulled the trigger and shot a hole in the water tower, and we went without water for five days. And you ain't had a bath since then!"

The posse laughed. The story was true at least the part about the water tower. Clark County had had some colorful characters in its earlier days, and some were still alive and kickin'. It was the local color that made the small town so unique.

"Sheriff," a man name Frank chimed in, "remember the time we time we jacked Curly's car up on blocks, just far enough off the ground so he couldn't tell the difference? When he came out of the pub, he started his car and accelerated through all the gears as if he was driving home..." Frank wanted to continue the story, but the crowd's laughter stifled it.

Sheriff Barnes could barely contain his deep, Southern drawl and belly laugh. "No more," he said. "I reckon we won't confront anything we can't handle, including an ornery polecat or two. Besides, most of you are scarier than any wildcat hiding out there." Again, the posse roared.

It was easy to see why Barney was a local celebrity. The city fathers often wondered why he'd stayed there so long, since he probably could have gotten a law enforcement job in any big city or be elected to some state office if he were so tempted. The city council wondered if he would be interested in being mayor—though, of course, that would be only after the current mayor decided not to run for another term.

"Are there any questions before we load up?" inquired the Sheriff "I've alerted Doc Madison of our itinerary and asked her to be ready just in case."

Now, some thought that Doc Madison would be a better horse doctor than a people doctor. Her bedside manner and language were more fitting for the barnyard than the hospital. But, she was good doctor to man or beast.

"Let's all keep an eye open for any signs of these kids," Barney concluded. "They could be anywhere along the road or in the ditch." His voice trailed off. Hearing no response, he directed the posse to follow his lead, and his thoughts turned to the task at hand. Would they find the three children? Would they still be alive? He had to exhibit *confidence* before his searchers, but he felt something else inside. He wanted to believe that all would end well, but the unresolved deaths of two men still haunted him.

"Mount up!" he boldly commanded his volunteers, and then pulled out with his trusting legions close behind.

11

Mickey and Stu studied the wheel tracks from the truck in which Breathe had been abducted. They followed the imprints of the tire treads as if they were walking a tightrope, often looking up, hoping that she would be waiting for them with her hands on her hips and that skewed look on her face.

"I sure wish Othello was here. She would find her with no problem," Stu said with a sigh. "Yup," chimed in Mickey.

The boys could not look at each other. They had never been in a situation like this before, but they felt each other's pain. Was she alive? they wondered. Had the men hurt her? What if they...?

The quiet was deafening. A northern breeze invaded their privacy and sent chills down their backs. Droplets spit upon them, bigger and then smaller. The wind swirled about and created a whistling sound through the trees. Dust devils frolicked ahead of them, almost teasing them. The sparrows dove at them from their high-wire lookout and then retreated back to safety.

But nothing seemed to bother the boys—not hunger, thirst,

rain or the chills. Breathe was their focus and nothing was going to stop them from finding her.

"If they hurt her, they'll get it from me," threatened Stu. His eyes moistened and his walk became more measured.

"Stu, we'll get through this," said Mickey. "We've been in tough situations before and come out alright." He knew he had to stay strong for both of them, and for Breathe. Stu was like a younger brother to him and Breathe—well; he liked her as more than just a sister. A lot more. And he thought she liked him equally.

They looked backwards and sideways to be sure that nobody was following them. The continual whine of the wind played tricks on their minds.

"What was that?" questioned Stu, almost stumbling over his own feet as he pirouetted. "Ah, it's just the wind." Mickey responded.

Both thought then that they heard two truck doors shut, one after the other. They listened intently, holding their breath. But only the thumping in their chests could be heard.

"Look!" exclaimed Mickey. He raced to a point alongside the road and picked up a yellow hair barrette. It was Breathe's. It was the one she had worn the morning they'd left on their trek.

"See!" exclaimed Mickey. "We're on the right path. She left us a signal." He handed the barrette to Stu. "You keep this as a good luck charm. We'll find her and she will be ok." He tried to inspire courage in Stu, but his voice tightened.

They walked a bit faster now, with newfound hope propelling them. They looked along the ditches for any additional fortunes. Who knows what would lead them next? Would it be a shoe or a piece of cloth? They were twin sentinels, on guard and edgy.

As they trudged through the wet road, the clay stuck to their tennis shoes and made their feet thicker, wider and heavier. Their legs ached and they began to tire. Stu squatted at the edge of the road and Mickey joined him. They panted, and then both broke into laughter as they looked at each other for the first time.

"We sound like Othello," said Mickey.

"Yeah," Stu agreed. "Now we know how she feels when *she's* tired." "Except, we don't have tails to wig-wag."

As each put an arm around the other, as if to offer courage and support, the sun broke through the grey cloud cover. The warmth felt good and gave relief to the scouts. The sun's rays streaked across the meadow and bounced off a silvery object ahead of them. It caught Mickey's eye, and he reeled toward Stu. "Did you see that?" He asked, standing up and beginning to run toward the silver piece. Stu jumped up and followed him. Suddenly, all their aches and pains evaporated.

In the middle of the road was a belt—well, sort of. Mickey pulled it from the muck. It *was* a belt, with a sliver buckle, but not Breathe's, nor any human's. It was a dog collar. Etched on the silver plate was, "Othello Lear, my noble friend." They looked at each other. Their hearts sank and sank.

"Oh, no," cried Mickey. For the first time, he let his emotions out. "If they hurt my dog, I'll..." He clutched Othello's collar and rubbed the silver tag. Stu took the collar, wiped the mud off it and gave it back.

Mickey had sent Othello home for help. Had she not obeyed? She'd always obeyed commands before. She was well-trained, but she was a guard dog, too. She was a German shepherd with noble bloodlines.

Mickey knew that Breathe and Othello had a special bond— they liked each other and everyone knew it when they saw them together. Mickey hoped that someday, he might have the same bond with Breathe.

"I bet Othello followed the kidnappers," offered Stu.

A faint cry broke their thoughts. It came from the cottonwood grove across the road. A large, marshy pond separated them from the sound. They listened and looked, but the ground fog interrupted their search. Was it just the wind, or killdeers swooping down on them? They looked at each other and then behind them. Nothing.

"There it is again. Did you hear that?" whispered Stu. "Shhhhhh!" demanded Mickey as he placed a finger to his lips.

Another faint cry floated from the grove. The boys strained their eyes and ears—still nothing. Their senses were on high alert and their skin crawled from the tops of their head to their toes. As they crouched and waddled across the road and down the edge, Mickey put Othello's collar in his back pocket. They continued on, stealthily moving to the bottom of the embankment, cautious not to bring attention to them. Mickey motioned to Stu to follow him and again put a finger against his lips.

They parted the tall grass, trying not to arouse any suspicion. Mickey motioned that he was going left and that Stu was to circle to the right. They moved cautiously.

"Help... Help me!" cried a familiar, female voice. The sound grew stronger as the boys flanked the thicket, drawing on their Boy Scout training. They had read about this tactic and practiced it; now, it was for real. They signaled *each* other until the tall grasses swallowed them.

Stu took another step and then fell face-down in some muck. His arms sank up to his shoulders and his chin barely stayed above the water line. He choked. He tried to rise to his knees, but the cattails grabbed his legs, and down he went. *Kerplunk!*

As he raised his head and gasped for air, he looked like an inhabitant of the swamp. Green slime slid from his ears and dripped off his chin. He wanted to rub the gunk from his eyes, but he couldn't free his arms and settled for rubbing his cheek on his shoulder. He was stuck! He spit brown water from his mouth, and his nose drained like a faucet.

Stu was afraid of water, and had never taken swimming lessons. *Too late now! he* thought.

"Drat!" he muttered as he struggled right himself. "What a fine mess you're in now."

Mickey was making his way to the left. He looked like an alligator as he crawled along the edge of the bog, mimicking a soldiers' crawl he'd seen in a war movie. A stinging feeling caught his attention and he rolled over to find himself atop a red ants' nest. The army attacked him, penetrating his clothes, and he swatted at them. This was not the war he'd seen on television. He was supposed to win!

The ants bit, crawled, and bit some more. They raced through his hair and entered his ears. He rolled and rolled, and in his haste, he forgot about the pain in his ankle. He also let go of his shotgun.

Splash! He dove into the murky slough and buried his head under *the water.*

"Ughhh", he gasped as he came back up, his face breaking the surface of the water. Chunks of mud trailed off his head. He gagged and swallowed, but it burned all the way down. He recognized the odor that he had often smelled when his dad and he *had* driven past similar sloughs. His dad had often talked about the smell of money, but this was not that kind of smell.

By that point, the silence was deafening, with only the gurgle of pond water trickling around a mud-piled beaver hut breaking the stillness. Mickey wanted to get up and charge toward the girl's now—faint cries, but his instinct told him not to.

12

The posse arrived at the bend in the road that overlooked the deserted hamlet. They dismounted from their iron horses and gathered at the back of the sheriff's horse trailer. Barney provided the instructions.

We will form two groups of four. The first group, led by Bob, will go along *the* sliver mine road, and I will lead the other team. We'll sweep the area along the cemetery. Keep on the lookout for anything—a piece of cloth, footprints, candy wrappers—anything! We'll meet at the old courthouse in one hour. If either group sees anything, Bob or I will fire one rifle shot into the air. Are there *any* questions?"

They took up their walking sticks and backpacks, assembled into their teams, and headed out.

Bob's team coursed its way down the mountain slope, avoiding the buck brush that pulled at their legs. The excitement of a quick resolution soon gave way to the arduous task of parting the tall weeds in front of them. The uncertain terrain jostled their steps and occasionally one man would stumble and fall, and the rest would stop and lift the searcher up. As they went on, their steps slowed and their breathing increased. The stops became more frequent and the energy waned, and the group's repartee was replaced by intermittent, incoherent grunts.

Meanwhile, Barney's pilgrims finally arrived at the edge of the cemetery, near the part assigned to non-citizens, primarily the Orientals who had worked the mines or performed menial jobs in the town. The group surveyed the sacred field, now choked by tangled weeds and populated with rows of sunken beds. A rare, wooden cross, or its remnant, left its mark.

Over there," one of the men in the party shouted. "Look! What is that?"

The sheriff and his group followed him over to a grave that had been disturbed. Dirt had been piled on several gravesites on both sides. The men moved closer, and Barney knelt down and picked up what appeared to be a plant.

"Marijuana," he said, nodding and looking up at *his crew*. "Someone's been opening graves and hiding marijuana in the cemetery. This must be the collecting site."

They looked at each other. Now it began to make sense. There had been rumors of strangers coming into town from time to time, but they never stayed very long they mostly came to buy gas and groceries. The vehicles they drove did not have license plates, and had darkened windows; these people rarely talked to anyone but when they did, they were polite and well-spoken. They were presentable, and looked just like normal folks on vacation with their families—though some appeared as husbands and wives, and some were alone.

Everyone in the search party thought back to the last time they had met one of these strangers. Had these unknown but friendly people been a part of this?

"Look at this," said Wally, breaking the silence. He bent down and clutched a handful of dirt, forming it into a ball. He handed it to the sheriff. "Barney, this dirt is wet. This grave was recently invaded. And here are some tracks." He pointed to a set of parallel, deep ruts nearby where some tires had left marks in the clay. They were wide, with deep treads and the kind of tires that were used for off road excursions.

The group walked around the pile of dirt, being careful to respect the open pit. As they inspected the graveyard, they saw evidence of recent digging, similar to the first excavation. Field grass had been matted down in two parallel paths from the cemetery to the access road—an area that had obviously been traveled often with heavy loads and been scarred by ruts.

Barney pulled his .30-06 from its scabbard. "It's time to regroup," he commanded.

At the same time, Bob's team was meandering down the hillside, where they came upon a neatly—maintained clearing. Row upon row of what appeared to be green-tufted turnip tops populated the acreage. Garden hoses snaked along the rows, each serpentine length connected to an above-ground, metal, stock pond filled *with* brown-colored water.

Starting at the top of the sloping hill, shiny, silver rivulets trickled along the furrowed trenches, carrying sustenance to each plant. Empty, plastic bottles that had once contained plant fertilizer lay in small piles at the end of each row. A heap of brown burlap bags and bundling twine was tucked under a hastily erected lean-to of scrap lumber and tarp. Small, tin cans and food wrappers decorated the native sagebrush and boot prints stamped the dirt in no certain pattern. In short, the place looked like a dumping ground.

"It's like finding an oasis," said Wally. "Unless you stumbled on it, you would never find it."

"So, this how they grow that funny weed," said another one of the men, smirking.

"Yup," agreed another. "You read and hear about it, but you never think it's in your own backyard. I thought farming was about potatoes, wheat, and hops."

The foursome walked along the plot, looking for signs of habitation. They found a small, circular arrangement of stones and blackened shards of wood. Bob placed his left hand above the pit.

"It's still warm," he said. "Somebody was here not too long ago. We need to find Barney and tell him what we've discovered."

Bob cocked his .30-30 Winchester and fired a single report into the sky, then told the rest of the group, "Let's head for the courthouse and meet up with the others."

Othello, who had searched ahead of the party, led them now toward the rendezvous.

13

Stu felt a sudden tightening around his neck. It burned, and he struggled to breathe. He gasped. He choked. His head felt hot and he saw stars. His body fell forward into the muck again.

"Lookin' for your sweetie, are ya?" said a strange voice.

Jake, the tall, skinny man from the pickup truck, grabbed Stu's legs and pulled him. He removed the bailing twine from Stu's neck, revealing a crimson scrape, and then used it to tie Stu's hands behind his back. He rolled the boy over and likewise secured his feet, then sat him up, retied some twine around his neck and secured it to the binding around Stu's hands.

"That'll hold ya," Jake growled as his small but well-built figure knelt over Stu and slapped him several times on the back of his head. "This'll teach ya not to mess in somethin' that's none of yer business. You're lucky I just don't kill ya here an' now."

Then, Jake pulled a machete out of a makeshift holster on his hip and placed the sharp edge under Stu's left ear. He moved the blade up and down the boy's jaw line, nicking his earlobe on an upward stroke. Dark-red blood streamed downward under Stu's collar.

Jake grabbed a handful of Stu's hair and snapped his head back. "You ain't even old enough to shave yet and you may not ever get there," he threatened. His sinister laugh hurt more than the cut, and his breath stunk worse than the scum floating on the nearby pond water.

Just then, Johnny, Sake's burly partner, ran over, pushing Stu's torturer aside and knocking the machete from his hand. "What are you doin'?" he shouted. "Are you crazy? We have to meet the boss at Hunter's Point and you're doin' this! Do you want to go back to prison? Jake, are you a fool? The last time you lost your mind, you ended up doing three to five. Do you want to go back there?"

The two stared at each other until Jake backed down.

"Don't push me, Johnny," he said, holstering his long blade. "Just don't push me or else."

The two men grabbed Stu under his armpits and dragged him along the slough's edge. Stu tried to resist, but with his extremities shackled, he was no match for the two thugs.

The three came to a small clearing where the pickup was parked. The men threw Stu to the ground and then moved to front of the truck. They cussed and pushed each other, their voices rising and then becoming inaudible. Their tussle moved them further away from the pickup and out of sight.

But then, there was a whisper. "Who's there?" said a voice that he immediately recognized as Breathe's. "Is there anybody there? Is that you Mickey? Stu?"

Stu rolled to his side and propped himself up against the truck's tire to try to get a better look.

Inside the back of the pickup, Breathe strained at her bonds. Her legs were buried under bales of burlap; she kicked at them, but to no avail. She squirmed and wiggled, her mind screaming with determination. Slowly, in excruciating pain, she inched her way to the end of the truck's box.

Hanging her head over the tailgate, she peered out and saw a figure on the ground. It had long, black, stringy hair and mud streaks across its cheek, and a reddish-blue color on its neck. It reminded her of a scarecrow *she* had put up as a decoration in her front yard one Halloween. But, this one was different: It uttered a sound.

"Yes," it said, its voice muffled by the constriction around its neck. "It's Stu." "*Shhhhhhhhhh!*" replied Breathe. "Keep *your* voice down_"

"Are you ok? Did they hurt you?" Stu asked.

Breathe let out a whimper, followed by a controlled sob, and then there was silence. She was tough—she'd never walked away from a fight, not even a fight with boys. She had wanted to play football, but the school officials would not allow it. They'd been concerned for her safety but what they didn't know was that Breathe could inflict and take more pain than most boys in her school, and all the boys knew it. But everyone had their limit, including her, and on this day, she had reached it.

"Breathe! Breathe!" said Stu. "If only Mickey and Othello were here, we'd get 'em." His voice trailed off. "I'll kill 'em," he muttered.

Breathe still heard the men arguing, and she just lay there, listening to the ranting. Her eyes closed and her head drooped. Even the short conversation had tired her out.

Stu's bindings scraped the skin from his wrists as he fought to free himself. "Mick, where are you?" he whispered frantically. "Othello?" He forced his head back, wincing in pain as the twine pulled against his wrists. It burned, and he could feel moisture oozing down his fingers.

"Breathe! Are you still with me?" he said. His vision blurred, and thought he saw something, but everything was moving and then he wasn't sure. Dizziness overcame him and he felt queasy. He heaved, his head aching, but nothing came up.

"Help me," he muttered as his chin rested on his chest.

Though Stu and Breathe couldn't see him, Mickey was crawling like a snake toward the edge of the slough, his appearance no better than Stu's. Upon reaching the edge, he scraped the willows and slime from his body. He regained his senses and parted the cat willows in front of him in an effort to fix his bearings, then moved toward the area where he'd last seen Stu.

The going was tedious as the thick, wet underbrush lashed at his ankles. The extra weight of the mud and debris slowed his trek, and the squishing inside his shoes forced him to walk more precariously. Bent and mashed weeds guided him toward what he hoped was a rendezvous with Stu. As he plodded along, he felt a pain jolt his left knee. He looked down and saw a strand of barbed wire hanging from his pant leg. It has lacerated his pants and punctured his skin. He moved on paying little attention to the sting of the barb.

Mickey knew he was on the right track, but where was Stu? And where was Breathe? What had happened to them? He reached into his back pocket and took out the Buck knife, opened it, and cut the wire from his pant leg. He tucked the weapon in his back pocket and moved forward.

Sneaking into some tall grass, he reached out and parted it with his hands, and his eyes set on what appeared to be a camp. Scanning the terrain, he saw a red gas can, and a small campfire flickering to survive. He heard voices, but he didn't see anyone.

A black pickup covered in military camouflage was parked near a clump of trees that protected it from detection from the gravel road. His eyes focused on a body leaning against the truck's rear tire, and he recognized the body's clothes-it was Stu! Mickey wanted to race to him, but his instinct told him not to, since the body wasn't moving.

Mickey continued to scout the encampment and spied a limp torso hanging halfway out of the pickup's box, tassels of straw-colored hair cascading down. He knew that hair—that was Breathe's? He was now about fifty feet away from his friends; they were all together again, minus Othello.

He looked for a rock to toss in their direction, but found nothing among the soggy cattail *shoots*. "Pssst... *Pssssssssssssst*," *he* risked, but there was no response. He wanted to cry out and run to them, but he knew that would jeopardize their lives—and his. And. he was their only hope.

14

The search party shared coffee and cookies in the center of town square. They leaned their backpacks against what remained of the picket fence. A couple of them removed their boots and rubbed their feet. Small talk ebbed and flowed among the posse as they speculated on what they had discovered.

"Well, you've all heard the findings of the two search teams," said the sheriff. "It appears that we have stumbled onto something bigger than we expected. We're lucky that we didn't meet the villains, but we're unlucky, so far, that we did not find the kids. But we will?"

There was general head-nodding amongst the party.

"How long have they been doin' this?" asked one of them.

Another inquired, "Why'd they dishonor the dead by diggin' up their graves and using them for hiding places for their evil deeds?"

"They ought to lock 'em up and throw away the key," offered a stout man, adding to the chorus of angry voices.

Bob stood up, dusted off his hat and began stowing his coffee cup and food wrappers. "I have as much anger and questions as you do, but let's stay focused on our task at hand. There will be plenty of time later to get answers to all our questions."

The others mumbled in agreement as they too stowed their gear, picked up their backpacks and reassembled.

"I've radioed back to the county dispatch for additional help," the sheriff told them. "My department is informing state authorities. I reckon they should be here shortly. In the meantime, we need to stick together and continue the search. Othello will lead us."

Barney's words seemed to calm and refocus the group.

Bob produced an item of Breathe's clothing from a plastic sack and stuck it in front of Othello's nose. Her tail wig-wagged, and she dashed back and forth among the group, encouraging them to follow her.

"She got the scent. Let's get goin'," ordered the sheriff.

The motley crew looked more like a band of nomads than a disciplined search party as they trudged along in irregular cadence. The late afternoon haze was interrupted by whimsical conversations unrelated to their reason for being there, but they helped break the tension. Often, Othello looked back at them as if to hasten them.

"Look," cried Chin at last, pointing at a white object streaming from a sage brush.

The nomads stopped abruptly and Chin darted down the embankment to retrieve the remnant, defying his old age and broken gait. He nearly rolled, but regained his balance. Two others followed, almost stumbling over each other in their excitement.

Chin plucked the strand and shared it with the other two. They laughed and patted each other on the back, then helped Chin scale the bank.

"It's just a plastic sack," Chin said with a chuckle as he waved *it* in front of the others. "Well, good eyes, Chin," mused Bob.

"Keep goin', Othello. Find 'em, girl," encouraged another teammate as the clan move on again.

"You go girl," offered an olive-complexioned woman.

A flirtatious whistle followed, and general laughter erupted. Others offered encouragement to Othello to drive on. The nomads were bonding. They picked up the pace, sensing that they were burning what daylight remained.

15

Mickey pulled the Buck from his pocket, careful not to slice himself. He severed a tall reed from its mooring and cut off both ends. He reached into to his shirt pocket and shook out a couple of the M&M candies he had been saving for a snack, one red and yellow. After inserting the red one into an end of the reed, he looked again at the encampment. He raised the reed to his mouth and pushed the front end of the make-shift blow gun through the cattails.

Whush! With *a* grunt, he exhaled as hard as he could into the weapon.

Boing! The red missile careened off the pickup's door. The two thugs who had been engaged in a heated discussion stopped and looked toward the truck.

"What was that?" said Johnny.

"Nothin'," retorted Jake. Your mind is messin' with ya' again. Be quiet or those two will hear us."

"Oh yeah? Well, I'm gonna mess up yer face if ya don't do

what I say," threatened Johnny. He grabbed Jake by the throat and the two of them wrestled to the ground, and rolled around in a death grip.

Mickey reloaded the reed and aimed it at Stu. *Whush! Splat!*

Stu's head snapped to the side. Mickey smiled, his yellow missile having found its target. He stowed the Buck and looked at the two wrestlers flopping around.

"Breathe," Stu said quietly. "Can you hear me? Mickey is here. Breathe!" He strained to see if she was alert, and then looked in the direction of the shot. He couldn't discern anyone as his eyeglasses had been smashed in the fight with his captors.

"Breathe," he whispered. "Breathe, Mickey is here. I can't see him. Can you?"

Breathe slightly lifted her head and looked toward Stu's voice. She mustered all the strength in her body to twist upward and strain her bonds. The pain was intense; a rib protruded from her side. She winced and softly moaned. Her whole right side was numb.

Mickey crept along the stand of reeds and moved toward his friends. He kept one eye on the two fools fighting and one eye on his footing. Now was not the time to trip and bring attention to himself. The wet grasses snarled his footsteps, but he applied what his father had taught him about how the Indians stalked their prey.

His efforts placed him in view of both the captors and his friends. He lay prone and crawled toward the pickup. Stu saw him and began contorting to free himself from his bindings. He motioned his head to the left, to alert Mickey of the location of the thugs_ Mickey put his index finger to his mouth and nodded in answer.

Stu then rolled his eyes to the right, trying to direct Mickey to Breathe's whereabouts. Again, Mickey responded that he knew. Mickey then maneuvered himself behind the pickup and looked into Breathe's face.

"Breathe," he whispered as he supported her head with his hand.

She responded with a rush of warmth through her body that brought new strength. She opened her eyes and offered a brief smile.

"Mick," she uttered.

"Shhhhh, it's gonna be alright. I'll get us out of here."
Mickey knelt so he could see how she was constrained in the
pickup bed, and he saw the blood-caked mud stuck to her side.
Anger rose in him and redoubled his resolve. He placed his hands
under her chest and pushed her body back into the truck's bed.
She winced, but did not spoke. She cried, but noiselessly. She
knew what he was doing, but it still ached.
Mickey moved to Stu's side then and pulled out the Buck knife.
He cut the twine around his arms, neck and feet. Stu rubbed his
wrists and ankles pushing blood back through his extremities. His
wrists and ankles burned where the bindings had been tied and thin
red drops oozed from the areas where the skin had been scraped.
"Thank goodness you're here. I knew you would come," he
gasped.
"You get Breathe and wrap her in your arms, and carry her
away from the truck to the trees," Mickey commanded. "She has
broken ribs and I don't know what else. Just be careful."
Stu nodded, and each of them moved in opposite directions,
toward their next tasks.
Stu cradled Breathe in his arms, careful not to inflict
additional pain. Breathe placed her arms around his neck. The
wrapped bales of contraband around her, wrapped in burlap, lay
heavily on her lower extremities. Her legs were pinned against the
side of the pickup bed from when she had attempted to extract
herself. He pulled her, and she began to cry.
"I need your help, Breathe," he intoned. "When I pull, you
need to push against the bales with your free leg. Ok?"
Meanwhile, Mickey had crawled lengthwise under the pickup
and was within six feet of the red gas can. He could see one only
one of the thugs. *Where's the other?* he thought. And then, he
froze. He looked back and saw Stu's feet and another two feet, but
they were not Breathe's! Had they been discovered?
"What do ya think you're doin'?" yelled Johnny from the back
of the truck. "Jake, get over here now!"
Johnny slugged Stu in the back of the head and he fell to the
ground. Breathe tried to help, but Johnny brushed her off. Jake
ran up and jumped on Stu, and retied his arms.
How did he get loose?" Johnny asked. "It's your fault we're in

this mess. I told you we should've gone back and run over the girl when she jumped from the truck. Instead, you wanted to keep her for ransom or something."

"Shut up," Jake retorted.

The two began arguing and pushing each other again, giving Mickey the break he needed. He rolled out from under the pickup and grabbed the gas can, and pulled it to the front wheel well. The can was more than half full, but he managed it. He squatted there for a moment, his heart pounding in his throat, as Johnny ordered Stu to his feet and forced him toward the slough.

"Enough of you," said Johnny. "Now, I'm gonna do what I should have done when I found you the first time."

"Where are you taking him?" Breathe shouted. "You leave him alone!"

"Shut up and say yer prayers," said Jake, slapping her hard across the face. She slumped down. Mickey could feel the sting of the slap from where he crouched.

Jake moved the bundles in the back of the truck, freeing Breathe's legs, and pulled her out of the bed and onto the ground. She landed with a thud; her body was like a rag doll. This tore at Mickey, as he could see her lifeless form. Jake left her there and went to see what Johnny was doing.

Now was Mickey's chance. He jumped to his feet and grabbed the gas can, then ran around the opposite side of the truck to avoid detection. He saw Breathe and pulled her to his side of the truck. He removed the cap from the gas can and began sprinkling its contents on the bundled merchandise. Then, he unscrewed the truck's gas cap and poured a trail of liquid from there to the edge of the trees.

Dropping the gas can, he came back and put Breathe over his shoulders, and carried her to the trees' edge. He put her down on the ground and shook her gently.

"Breathe, wake up," he said. "You need to help me save Stu." He shook her again and she barely opened her eyes. "Stu is in trouble and we need to save him, now," Mickey told her as he fumbled to take a pack of matches from his pocket.

She rolled onto her side and put her hands out, trying to pull herself up. With Mickey's help, she sat on her knees, and then she looked at him. A deep resolve pushed her. She took the matchbook from Mickey's hand and ripped half the matches from the fold. Her nervous hands shaking, she dropped the matches on the ground, but quickly picked them up before they became useless.

"When you hear me yell," Mickey told her, "I want you to light the gas trail on fire and then get into the woods as fast as you can. Don't look back—just keep going. We'll find you." His voice faltered as a cold rush come over him. "Or else someone will find you," he muttered under his breath. He hugged her and kissed her forehead, then hugged her again. She squeezed his hand and returned his kiss.

In a crouch, Mickey ambled in the direction that the men had taken Stu. He followed the broken reeds and cattails and the sunken footsteps; one set led the other and an occasional body imprint showed where one of the men had fallen. A deeper set of footprints followed them.

Before long, he heard voices arguing. As he approached a clearing, he saw the two thugs standing and Stu prostrate on the ground. Mickey moved back and around the glen. He inhaled deeply three or four times and then, with a mighty burst of energy, he roared at the top of his lungs and began running through the cattails and reeds. Birds took flight and field mice scurried for safety.

"Aaarrraaaaggghhh!" He repeated the roar again and again, the sound growing louder and throatier each time. He trampled back and forth through the bog back; he fell and righted himself.

In the meantime, Breathe struck the matches, and they crumbled. She tore more from the book and struck them, and they spawned into flame. She lit the small pile of twigs, and then turned to crawl toward the clump of trees, but her foot kicked up dirt and killed the fire. She squirmed back and picked up the strewn book of matches; only one match remained. Her heart sank.

What if... she thought, but then shook it from her mind and carefully struck the singleton. It erupted and as she touched the soaked path again, the fire raced along the thin line, toward its goal. She clamored to her feet and ran as fast as she could. She fell and writhed in. She got to her knees and crawled. She ached, but somehow she made it *to an obscure area.*

Seeing the distraction that Breathe had caused, Stu rolled out of sight and into the slough—his second trip there. A moment later, a large clap of what sounded like thunder erupted *from* the area in which the truck was parked. Johnny and Jake were startled.

"What the...?" Johnny muttered.

They looked in that direction to see a large mushroom of fire followed by a stream of billowing, black-and-white smoke. They ran toward the fire, forgetting about everything else.

In the slough, Mickey found Stu and lifted him from the muck, and wiped him off. He cut Stu's wrist restraints and lifted him up, supporting his weight. For once, Stu's small stature was a benefit.

"What took you so long?" Stu asked smugly.

"I had to round up all the animals in the jungle to help," Mickey said with a smirk. "Let's get Breathe and get out of here."

16

The truck and its cargo provided a magnificent display of fireworks. Breathe, the appointed arson, had done her job. As she, Stu and Mickey watched from a distance, it reminded her of when the high school would have a homecoming bonfire.

The flames from the pickup shot into the darkening sky, and plumes of smoke followed. The cab was fully engulfed in fire and an occasional bullet exploded. The cargo sent a white, sweet-smelling cloud rising upward and drifting with the prevailing wind. The truck's tires popped in celebration. Breathe watch with great satisfaction—and a sense of revenge.

Jake and Johnny carried hatfuls of slough water to the fire, in an effort to douse the cargo. They danced in contortions of disbelief as their prized possession went up in smoke, stumbling and often bumping into each other in their wild firefighting gyrations.

"What are we going to tell the big man?" Jake cried. "We're dead meat! They'll never believe this."

"We got to get out the country," said Johnny. "We'll never get away with this."

The two argued back and forth as they carried water to the blaze. They were, exhausted as they stood along side the raging fire. Large acrid plumes of smoke *fueled* by boring rubber tires billowed into the air. They were a dismal sight, two hollow spirits. They had thought this would be easy summer money to pay for college. Now, their futures were going to be moment-to-moment.

"We need to find those kids first," exclaimed Johnny. "They can identify us."

"Yeah," agreed Jake. "Maybe, if we find them, the big man will go easy on us. We can trade their hides for ours."

The two felt a sense of vindication. They stood up and looked around at the clump of trees atop the small knoll and at the slough below. None of the three children was visible.

"We need to split up," ordered Johnny. "You take the slough bottom and I'll take the tree line. We'll meet where the upper ridge drains into the slough." The two moved out to their territories, carefully looking back over their shoulders, anticipating a surprise attack. Eventually, they were out of sight of each other.

Mickey made his way around the slough and was startled to find Stu staring at him with that quaint smirk and cocked head. Mickey and Stu looked at each other and smiled. The nodded and headed for the grove of trees hoping to find Breathe—and hoping to find her alive.

"Breathe." they whispered. Stu nearly tripped over her as he stepped over a pile of branches. An arm reached out and grabbed S4 and he nearly screamed.

"Over here Mick." He motioned. They pulled her from the trappings and sat her up. "Now's our chance," she said.

"You stay here and we'll get 'em," replied Stu. Mickey nodded in agreement.

"No way!" Breathe protested. "I may be hurtin', but I'm not going to miss this for the world. I have dibs on the little jerk who slapped me around."

The boys could barely keep from laughing out loud. They had seen that look in her eyes before, and she was not to be denied. If Breathe did not get her way, she took it.

The three clenched their fists and bounced their knuckles off each other. They huddled together and Mickey laid out the plan. Then, they hugged each other and went to complete their assignments.

Johnny and Jake separately inched their ways to the ravine where they were to meet. One whistled, imitating a swallow, and the other responded likewise. But, little did they know that they, the trackers, were becoming the tracked: Breathe and Stu had made their way along the ridge to the top of the ravine as well, and were crawling to its edge, where they had a view of the small gorge and the slough at the bottom. Immediately deploying their part of the plan, Breathe scoured the area for some long branches as best she could, and Stu lost no time in foraging for a downed tree.

Meanwhile, Mickey had made his way around the opposite end of the slough, retracing the steps he had made earlier, on his way to find his friends. He listened to the occasional whistles and knew that he was maintaining his outer position from Johnny.

He stopped at the juncture where he had fallen on the ant pile. He removed his shirt and formed a makeshift sack, then scooped up a couple handfuls of sand, containing the tiny red creatures, and dumped them inside. He folded the top and the shirttails over and tied the sleeves across, forming a perfect sack. He then pulled out the Buck knife and cut a couple of green will poles, shearing the leaves and nipping the ends.

Mickey moved rapidly then, outflanking the slower thug until he reached an opening where two animal paths bisected each other. There, he knelt and caught his breath.

Jake stumbled his way along the bog. His gait suggested that he had lost some zest for this game, and he looked downward rather than forward. He plodded on, whistling in response to Johnny's bird calls.

Stu finally found what he was searching for—a large log about ten feet long. It was devoid of branches and leaves; it had fallen long before. He motioned Breathe to his find, and the two agreed upon the plan to move it into position. They used the long braches Breathe had found and began rolling the log to within ten feet of the top of the ravine.

At the same time, Mickey stuck one end of the green willow deep into the mud along one side of the path, and stuck the other green willow on the other side of the path. He pulled out the Buck and cut some long strands of wet grass, and fashioned a cup by twisting the strands together. He then cut a wedge in the end of each pole and laced the ends of each with bark from the poles. He packed the cup with mud.

Sitting down on the path, he carefully drew the two poles to his waist and placed the folded shirt with its inhabitants into the homemade cup. He covered himself with the rest of the cut willows and reeds, blending into the foliage. Slowly, Mickey lay back until he was lying down, face up, in the path. And then, he waited.

On the other side of the slough, Breathe struggled to help move the log, but she and Stu got it to the ravine's edge. They took their posts and watched. Stu pointed to some movement below them. It was Jake.

"Help! Help me," cried Breathe. She repeated it, as had been predetermined. "I'm hurt and need help. I need a doctor. I'm thirsty!"

Jake was re-energized by the sound of her moaning. He looked up to see Breathe faintly waving her arms at him.

"Johnny, Johnny, I found her!" he hollered at the top of his lungs. "She's over here." He abruptly turned and headed up the ravine, grabbing at every shrub to steady his climb.

"Hurry! Hurry!" Breathe pleaded. "I'm bleeding and need a doctor."

Jake worked his way nearly to the top of the ravine.

"Shut up, Jake!" Johnny called after him. "Shut up! You're givin' our positions away. Stupid!" He then spun around and headed down the path that led directly to the ravine.

Kawhump! He had entered the kill zone. Mickey released the cup just as Johnny stepped into the spot where the two paths crossed. The sling worked flawlessly, hurling its payload; it unfolded and hit Johnny in the face and neck. The shirt wrapped around his head and its passengers and debris spread across his face, invading his mouth, eyes and ears. He fell onto his face and gagged. Mickey leaped on top of him, pushed his face into the ground and put the Buck knife to the back of his neck.

"One, two, three," said Stu and Breathe in unison, then used all their strength to pry the log toward the edge of the ravine. It gained momentum and speed as it careened down the ravine lengthwise, its end whipping sideways. Jake ducked, but the stub caught him on the shoulder and flipped him into the air. He tumbled in sync with the log, stopping at the bottom of the crevice with the log straddling his legs. He screamed in pain.

Stu raced down hill to the crash site with Breathe trailing behind as rapidly as she could. As Mickey heard Jake's cries, he lifted Johnny to his feet and pushed him to the bottom of the ravine.

17

The staggering plumes of black smoke rose like a broken chimney above the tree line and swept heavenward like strands of angel's hair. The tangerine glow of the setting sun accented its path. The posse pointed to its flight and tracked it to its origin.

"What is that?" questioned Jilly. She feared the worst, considering her experiences.

"It must be a grass fire, what with all the lightning we've had recently," interjected another woman.

"Let's head that way and check it out," said the sheriff. "We don't want to get trapped in its path with no way out."

"Maybe it was set on purpose," offered one of the men. "It might be a sign from the three kids, calling for help."

Othello pricked her ears, straining for a familiar voice. She turned her head in either direction, trying to pick up a scent—any scent. She barked at the group to follow her as she headed in the general direction of the smoke. The search party altered its course and hiked toward the bluff with the scout dog in the lead.

Othello barked again. She stopped in her tracks and sniffed the air.

"She's got something," cried Jilly.

Othello danced wildly around the posse. She raced ahead of them and back again as if dragging them forward.

"You go girl. Find 'em," ordered Bob.

Othello took flight and darted along the golden wheat field. The team followed as rapidly as possible. She stopped and sniffed again, consuming the air with small bites and nods of her head. She looked left and right, and then plunged headlong into the wheat field.

The posse followed. It was as if it was a child's game of tag, with the search party trying to catch the dog, except that she had the advantage of fours legs and being built lower to the ground. The party fell behind and Othello impatiently waited, then darted ahead.

"Othello, wait for us," commanded Jilly.

Othello abruptly stopped and waited for them.

"Let's take five," suggested a larger man.

"Good idea," agreed and older lady.

"You can if you want, but not me." Jilly responded. "Those kids are out here and who knows who has them or what." she argued.

We need to be careful here," he cautioned. "There have been reports of car lights and strange goings-on in this neck of the woods."

Jilly knew all to well what he was saying. It had been after one of these reports that Reynolds had left to investigate, and he had not returned alive. They'd said it had been an accident, but she knew better. If anything, he'd been too careful with everything, especially weapons. The thought that something was happening to Mickey made her shudder inside. She looked at Barney, not knowing that he had been looking at her all along.

"Best we keep movin'," he said.

Othello leaped to her feet and moved to the front of the pack. After all, she was the alpha dog. She sniffed the air and looked back, but waited for the others. Slowly, the team reassembled. Aches and pains began to set in again. This was not their normal routine on any given night.

As they drew up on a rise in the wheat field, they could see a dark object engulfed in fire and black smoke. At the top of the ridgeline, a petite figure was waving a banner of some sort. The rise gently dropped toward the slough.

"Look."

"Over there."

"I see someone on top of the hill. It's one of the kids."

They forgot about their tiredness and discomfort as the sighting energized them. Their arms flailed in the air attempting to get the attention of the figure on the hill. They whistled and called out their names. They raced out-of-control toward the burning inferno. The orderly search party has disintegrated into a mob.

Suddenly, a brood of pheasant hens took flight, scaring the searchers to death. They stopped dead and let their hearts settle down. Then, a big rooster followed. It was a mammoth bird, rising from the lodged stand of wheat. It had a splash of blue on it upper tail with red, brown and orange interspersed. It was huge—at least, to their startled eyes. It worked to gain altitude, glided and landed almost as quickly, scurrying along the underbrush with its harem.

"That is the biggest cock pheasant I have ever seen!" shouted Bob. "Look at it go. Have you ever seen such a beauty?"

"Did you see that one with the tail feathers?" responded a heavy-set man. "I bet that one would win the shotgun prize hands-down."

They watched to see if the sortie would take flight, coast back over the rise and set somewhere else in the grain field.

"If I only had my shotgun," lamented Chin.

"Gone for now, but we'll be back," promised the portly gentleman.

They followed the wild animal path along the slough until they came upon a matted area.

"Look," said Jilly. She ran into the bog and pulled a broken shotgun from the muck, and wiped it off. Barney followed close behind her.

"It's Mickey's! I'd know it anywhere," said Jilly. "His dad gave it to him. Where is Mickey? What happened to him?"

Barney put his arms around her and pulled her close to him. "We'll find him," he said. "We'll find all three. They'll be just fine."

They reassembled, and Othello led them along the matted path. She found a torn shirt, clenched it in her jaws, and ran directly to Jilly.

"'Othello! Drop," Jilly commanded. Othello released the shirt and sat at her side.

Jilly picked up the shirt and examined it. "This is Mickey's!" she announced. "He was wearing it this morning when he left with Stu. They were going meet Breathe and go pheasant hunting." She opened the muddied shirt and ants dropped from its insides. She shook it, scraped the mud and weeds from its trappings, and tucked in into her backpack.

They came upon an area where two poles stood vertically along each side of the path. From the imprints and compressed weeds, it appeared as though a scuffle of some magnitude had taken place. Bob picked up a grouping of reeds, noticing that the ends were cut cleanly.

Othello was waiting at the upward slope of the slough, barking loudly. Her animation suggested that she had found something of significance. The group groped their way up the slope and spotted the smoldering hulk of a vehicle. They skirted it and found a fire-blackened trail leading to the top of the ridgeline.

As their eyes aligned with the summit, they saw Breathe waving faintly to get their attention.

"Breathe, are you ok?" Jilly shouted as she raced toward the girl. They shrieked with joy and burst into tears and laughter. The tried to dance, but the wound in Breathe's side forced her to sit down.

"Where are the boys?" questioned Jilly.

"Are they all right? Where did you lat see them?" she begged.

Othello broke from the group and headed to the ridgeline. The search party followed the burnt path, arriving at the precipice, where the empty red gas can lay.

"Breathe, are you alright?" the sheriff asked the disheveled girl as they approached. Her hair was clumped with splotches of mud; her faced was a portrait of dried blood, brownish bruises and tear-stained tracks. Her cheeks were sunken and her eyes were deep-set. She leaned at an angle, as she could not stand erect, and she held her side with both hands.

Breathe's mother pushed her way through the crowd and draped her in a blanket, and held her gently in her arms. With much effort, Breathe raised her left arm and pointed in Stu's direction. He stood at the bottom of the ravine with Mickey and his captive.

"The other one is trapped under the log. It worked just as you had planned. I think he is badly hurt. He has a pulse, but eyes are closed and he didn't move when I shook him." answered Bob.

"Where is Breathe?" Mickey asked Stu.

"She saw a group of people headed our way, so she went back to the ridgeline to signal them."

Breathe and the rescue party stood above them, then descended the ravine and met the two boys and the two thugs. Jilly hugged Mickey, nearly choking him, and then repeated the affection with Stu. They all stood as if they were frozen. Nothing more was said; nothing more needed to be said.

18

The search party became a rescue party as they aligned themselves along the log, placing stout poles, cut from tree limbs, under the log.

"On three, we'll pry the log loose and drag this sorry soul out," directed Bob as he motioned the party to place their leverages.

No sooner had they set their pry bars than the county fire truck, with its red lights ablaze, rumbled across the field, weaving its way toward the smoldering hulk. Grasping the handrails on each side were six firemen dressed in reflective, fire-retardant suits, complete with protective helmets. The truck plowed deep furrows and flung chunks of stalk and dirt clumps from under its running boards as it careened across the broken field. It stopped short of the bog, and the passengers alit and raced to the ravine.

The firemen carried ropes, axes and portable fire extinguishers. Four of them ran to the smoking remains of the pickup and doused its carcass. The other three rapidly ascended the ravine to provide assistance in saving the trapped thug.

"One, two, three," yelled Bob, grunting in unison with the others. Still, the log refused to budge.

"Jilly! Get that coward over here," demanded Barney, pointing to Johnny. "He can help save his buddy."

Jilly motioned to Johnny, who was lying on the ground in a curled-up contortion, to get up and help the others. She untied his wrists and pushed him in their direction. Othello nipped at his ankles as he walked over, and Jilly stayed on point, guarding him like he was her prisoner.

"One, two, three," commanded Barney. Again, the log didn't budge.

"You guys come over here. We need your help," hollered the fire chief, waving frantically at the four firefighters who had already completed their assignment.

With the efforts of the combined teams, the log lifted momentarily, allowing the stout searcher to reach under Jake's shoulders and pull him from the entrapment. Jake screamed with a shrill pitch that so startled the group, they dropped the log, barely missing some of the rescuers' toes. The log slid, stopped and pitched lengthwise. They jumped out of the way as the dirt underneath let loose and the log began rolling down the ravine.

The ambulance stopped abruptly to avoid the log as it spun across its path. The back window and tailgate opened and two males dressed in white clothes jumped out. They were carrying suitcases–like boxes.

Two firemen unfolded a canvas stretcher and several assisted in securing Jake to it. He was awake, but he lay motionless. One of the emergency technicians gave him and injection that put him to sleep while the other technician inserted a needle into his forearm. Fluid flowed from a pouch, through a tube and into his body. The firemen transported him to a station wagon that had been converted into the county's ambulance. Once he was loaded, the vehicle slowly gained traction and sped across the field, toward the gravel road.

"Look out! Get out of its way," yelled several members of the search party as they stumbled and tripped over each other, getting out of the ambulance's path. Two of the mercenaries tumbled down the ravine, accompanying the log to its resting place, moored in the muck of the slough. They regained their feet, staggered about briefly, and then waved to the others, signaling that they were not injured.

Johnny looked about and saw this commotion as an opportunity to escape. No one was watching him as he backpedaled from the remaining group. He turned and ran, as fast as his legs could carry him, parallel to the ridgeline, ducking down so as not to be seen. Just as he almost gained his freedom, he was hit from behind by a four-legged pursuer.

"Owwwwwww," he yelped as Othello sunk her teeth into the back of his leg and locked her jaws. The two of them rolled halfway down the sloping hill. Johnny tried to kick the dog off, but her teeth were deeply embedded in his flesh.

Othello was enjoying this too much. She stood over him, shaking her head viciously to the left and then to the right, clenching his torn flesh in her jowls. Blood soaked through his pants and combined with the soil and Othello's saliva to form a muddy paste. Though several people ran to Othello's aid, she continued to tug at her prize, trying to pull it in the opposite direction. It was like the game of tug-of-war Mickey and she always played: he would give in and then pull back; Othello would pull back and then give in, only to trick Mickey into relaxing so she could steal the rope. She won more times than she lost, as was the verdict here.

"Drop, Othello, drop," ordered Mickey. Othello released her prey and heeled. Blood and spit drooled from her mouth as she sought favor from Mickey. He obliged by petting her and reinforcing her good behavior. Breathe and Stu came over and gave Othello hugs, with Breathe promising her a treat when they got home.

"Ya got what ya deserved," the sheriff said to Johnny. "You're lucky we called her off when we did or ya'd be a goner. She likes leg steak." The group roared with approval.

"Barney, maybe ya can make this situation into cowboy

poetry and enter it at the county fair," offered one of the men from the search party.

Yeah, and I bet this guy would be the first to vote for ya," added another. Again, they all roared with delight.

"Get up," demanded Barney, lifting Johnny to his feet. As he did so, a gold medallion fell from Johnny's pocket. Bob stooped and picked it up. It was in the shape of a shield with the numbers 45729 etched on the top. Further inspection revealed the raised inscription "Silverton County Game Warden." Bob looked at Barney, and they turned to Jilly. They both had a sick look about them. They walked toward her and gave her the badge. She gasped.

"Oh, no!" she cried. "It's Reynolds'!"

She clutched the badge to her chest and looked for Mickey. Barney comforted her by holding her in his arms as Mickey approached. She pulled back from Barney and gave the golden shield to her son.

"It was your dad's," she said.

"I know," he replied.

Barney turned back to Johnny. "You are under arrest for the murder of Reynolds Stellon. You have the right to remain silent, the right to an attorney. If you cannot—"

"Yeah, yeah," interrupted Johnny as he tried to free himself from the handcuffs Bob had placed on his wrists. "If he hadn't been so nosy, he'd still be alive. He just kept snooping around. Got what he deserved."

Breathe and Stu touched Mickey. There were times for words and times for feelings, and this was the latter. They could smell it in the air and taste it as well. Neither was good.

Now everybody would know the truth and what they had believed all along—that Reynolds had *not* died by accident—nor had he taken his own life, as suggested by some of the town yokels. They had been quick to judge and so cruel in their slander. But, that was a story for a different time and place. Now, it was Jilly's and Mickey's turn to pick the time and place to tell the real story, if they chose to lower themselves to that ilk's level.

"Time to go!" Barney shouted, his voice shattering the calm and bringing the mourners back to the here and now.

After securing their gear—including the accused—the posse and the firefighters boarded the fire truck. The big diesel engine roared to life.

"Mom, I want to start walking back to the old mining town," Mickey said. "There's plenty of daylight. I want to sort something out in my head. You can pick me up on the way into town. You have to come back on this road anyway."

Jilly hesitated, but did not resist.

"And I'm *going* to walk with Mickey," added Breathe. Her mother, although more controlling, led her to the fire buck where the medical technicians attended to her wounds. They assisted in lifting her into the back of the fire truck for the ride back to town.

"Me too," said Stu. Jilly nodded as if approving for Stu's parents.

Othello barked, and Jilly couldn't help but smile. ""Yes, you too," she replied.

The fire truck inched its way away from the three figures, straining under its cargo. Slowly, it gained traction and ground its way toward the gravel road. They waved to each other. The quiet was deafening. Mickey and Stu looked back at the blackened metal mass and scanned the ridgeline until their eyes focused on the slough. That was where the plan had come to life.

"Let's go home," said Mickey with a sound of relief in his voice.

They backtracked across the amber-colored field with Othello leading the way, as usual. They realized that they were hungry. And they were thirsty. And they were tired. They felt all these at the same time, but there was a stronger bond amongst them. Each felt this more than anything else.

"Look! Look at this," said Mickey, picking up a long pheasant feather that had been riding on the grain. It was brown and tan with some teal coloring, and it was long—very long. Mickey was excited by his find, as were his compatriots. He stroked the length of the feather and felt its soft texture. He shared his find with the others and they shared in his delight as they made their way to the gravel road.

He twirled the feather in his hand and tossed it into the air.

He watched it float to the ground and then retrieved it. *This will look great mounted on my bedroom wall*, he mused. He held the feather like a spear, aimed it at Breathe and launched it at her. It bounced off her shoulder. They all laughed.

"Musta been a bird that needed support like that," suggested Stu as he tried to hold a straight face.

"Yeah, musta been a B-52," replied Mickey, mimicking Stu's stoic look.

The boys spread their arms, emulating B-52's as if their arms as if beginning a bombing sortie. They tried to imitate a plane's roaring engines but sounded more like soprano spitfires. Othello got caught in the frolic and jumped at the two aviators.

"You guys are both sick," said Breathe. "Where did you get that sense of humor?" It was the comic relief they needed to rekindle their inner lights and reawaken their childhoods.

Breathe shook her head and kicked at a round stone in the road. It bounced in front of them and nearly struck Othello. Breathe then selected a flat, small stone and hurled it horizontally, skipping it across the placid stock watering pond adjacent to the road. The stone bounced, bounced and bounced again before it sank. The boys cheered and whistled, then picked up stones and joined in the challenge to see whose discus could skip the most times.

"One, two, ohhhhhhh," lamented Stu as his launch fizzled.

"Watch this! I can do better than that." Mickey laid the feather on the roadway, leaned back and flung his entry. "One, two, ohhhhhhhh no," he cried as his stone nosedived into the pond. Othello barked at every splash.

The three laughed and began throwing rocks to see who could throw one the farthest. Small stones were soon replaced with bigger rocks, and small ripples were replaced by bigger ripples until petite waves rolled into the pond's edge.

"Too much fun, way too much fun," stated Mickey as he rubbed his elbow.

They journeyed on the road to town, anticipating that their ride would be forthcoming.

"Oh, my feather." Mickey turned back to see Othello trotting behind them, carrying the monstrous feather lightly in her mouth.

Upon Mickey's command, she released the feather and received a pat on the head.

"Mickey, I think you should enter the feather in the contest," said Breathe. "I bet you'd win the shotgun hands-down. Don't you agree, Stu?" She looked to Stu for support.

"Yeah, and it would teach all those big-city hunters a lesson," Stu agreed.

"Yeah, but I didn't shoot no bird and I don't got the bird to show for it, either," lamented Mickey.

They walked side by side, giving the appearance of a Revolutionary War trio, absent the decorum and trappings of that era. A hawk swooped down from its high-wire perch and nabbed a small field mouse, then returned to its nest. A brown, furry badger waddled across the road within fifty feet of the three and ducked into the underbrush on the other side. They ran to see if they could catch it. Othello, being the fastest of the four, failed to keep pace with the fur ball.

Ya know, I don't remember the rules saying anything about having to bring in the bird that the feather came from. Did you?" Breathe had that quizzical look about her. The three looked at each other and shrugged.

"I dunno," said Stu.

"Can't remember," said Mickey.

The prize that they had capriciously tossed about now took on new value. It was priceless, fragile, and deserved a safer place than on Mickey's bedroom wall. Neither Breathe nor Stu had any desire to transport the great find. They were satisfied to be guardians rather than bearers.

"Let's do it," smirked Mickey. "Let's enter it into the contest and see what happens. The worst they can do is say 'no.'" Their steps were reinvigorated—a pace Othello preferred all along.

From the rolling dust ahead, they surmised that their ride home was moments away. They moved to the side of the road and ordered Othello to heel. As the caravan approached, the two boys reached out with their thumbs as if they were hitchhiking, and Breathe slightly lifted her pant leg. The pain of her wound still ached, but she was too tired to feel it.

"All aboard," exclaimed one of the firemen.

"Breathe, you better ride up here with us so there is room for the boys," suggested her Mother. The boys jumped onto the back of the fire truck. Othello was not going to be left behind—she jumped in second.

They all settled in the back and listened to the grind of the tires on the gravel road and the sound of an occasional rock pinging off the undercarriage. They were too tired to comprehend what they had just experienced, but they were going home, finally.

19

Mickey could smell the aroma of bacon as it drifted throughout the house and into his bedroom, teasing his nostrils. The sizzling and popping sounds further tantalized his ears until he could not stand it anymore.

He risked opening one eye to see if it was really morning. Then, the second eye opened slightly. A streak of sunlight penetrated the window coverings and struck him squarely in the face. He rolled over and plopped the pillow over his head.

It had been a mere two days since his adventure with Stu and Breathe and he had not yet set foot outside the house. Today, Othello had tried several times to rouse him, pulling the covers off his crumpled form, but, it had been no use. The bedding had found its way back, wrapping the mummy more tightly.

"Mickey," Jilly called. "Time to rise and shine." She knocked on the bedroom door and cracked it open. "Do you know what day it is?" she asked as she snapped the light switch on. Immediately, an explosion of light engulfed the room and Mickey knew it was time to get up. He sat up in bed and moaned. Every bone and muscle in his body clamored for relief.

"I think I've been hit by a truck," he moaned as he threw the blankets back and slowly set his feet on the floor. He didn't even mind the coolness of the linoleum as it provided momentary relief. He tried to stand up, but sat back down abruptly. His muscles cried out and he responded in kind.

"Are you sure you are ok? I know you are tough, but you three have been through a lot today," Jilly asked him as she gathered his clothes that were piled in the corner.

Mickey was too tired to answer, but nodded.

After a long shower that temporarily drained the hot water resources, Mickey dressed, ambled to the kitchen table, and plopped himself in a chair. It was a hard landing, for his legs had not recovered enough to cushion the shocking descent. He petted his dog and nodded to his mother.

"I'm so hungry, I could eat a horse," he said, reaching for a strip of bacon, but he retracted his hand as Jilly sat with her hands folded. They prayed, but he grabbed for the bacon again before "amen" was even said.

Jilly smiled, and he smiled. Othello barked, as she wanted her share of breakfast. After all, she worked hard, too.

"Do you know what day it is?" Jilly asked for the second time.

Mickey stared at her and nodded his head. "It's the last day to enter the longest feather contest," he replied with a sense of urgency in his voice. "I got to call Stu." He asked if he could be excused from the table, but Mom motioned for him to stay seated. He looked at her quizzically look. "What?" he deadpanned. He was itching to get moving.

"Today is Father's Day and I would like to take a few minutes to remind you of what a good husband and dad he was to both of us. She shared a story about how, one day when the local store had been closed, they had been out of milk and Mickey had been crying. So, Reynolds had driven to the big city and returned with the staple.

Jilly lifted her napkin and picked up a gold, shiny object.

"Dad would want you to have this, I'm sure," she said. Her voice trembled and her hands shook slightly as she placed Reynolds' badge in Mickey's hand. They both looked at the present, fearing looking at each other.

"Perhaps you will follow in his footsteps," Jilly said.

The pain of sitting there was greater than the pain Mickey's body had felt earlier. He rose and gave his mother a big hug, exchanging their love for each other. The embrace was broken by a wet nose prying between them and a slight breeze caused by the wig-wag of the intruder's tail.

"Be sure to call Breathe," Jilly said as Mickey got up from the table. "She wanted to go with you and Stu."

Othello was prancing at the front door. She was not going to be left out. Mickey put on his windbreaker and donned his favorite camouflage cap. He wanted to be seen as a hunter among hunters, and not as just some kid. He strung a knife sheath on his belt, loaded with the knife he had acquired from the tall thug, Johnny. It was his spoil of war.

"See ya, Mom," he called as he and his best friend bolted out the front door. He stuck his head back in to remind her that if either of his buddies called, she should tell them he would meet them on the way to the drug store. The door slammed, but opened again. Mickey sheepishly went to his room and took the feather from its hiding place. He waved it at his mother and gave that bright smile that too often reminded her of his father. She shook her head and smiled back. The door slammed shut again.

20

The sun rose brightly in the limitless sky. Its fiery orb contrasted sharply against the azure canvas, its solar rays carrying welcome relief as the heat penetrated Mickey's sore muscles.

Today was special. He looked at the feather, but his trance was interrupted by two familiar voices—ones he would recognize anywhere. Othello barked and ran ahead to greet the two fellow warriors. They all stopped to share pleasantries and give each other hugs and knuckle greetings. Mickey offered to let Breathe carry the feather. It was his way of acknowledging her purple heart. She had been the one wounded in the battle, so to speak.

"How's your ribs?" he inquired as he reached for her hand. She met his halfway with a squeeze. This was a form of communication that did not require words.

"Othello, will you hold my hand?" said Stu with a laugh, and he slapped Mickey on the back and jogged ahead to avoid any repercussions. He knew what payback was like.

As they walked along Main Street, they were greeted with

applause and whistles from citizens passing by. Words of congratulation filled the air as they passed the local farmers' market in the town square. Many locals stopped what they were doing and pointed at the foursome.

The three kids looked at each other and shrugged. The grocer reached out and shook their hands, offering each a shiny, red apple. Ladies smiled and nodded in approval. Children playing in the street pointed at them and then went back to kicking their soccer ball.

"Wow! Look at the crowd," gasped Breathe as they approached the front of Walser Drug. She returned the feather to Mickey, fearing that something bad might happen to it. They pushed toward the front of the throng, jostling and picking any opening that advanced their efforts. Multiple conversations created a humming chorus among the attendees. Heads craned to see the front of the store.

"Five minutes 'til the contest closes," barked the druggist. His rotund body easily projected his deep, gruff voice. His reading glasses balanced on the end of his bulbous nose and the distance between that landmark and his high forehead was punctuated by continuous row of thick eyebrows. His black hair—what remained of it—was flipped from just above his left ear over to the other ear. The kids loved to watch him walk on windy days, as his hair would lift and a shiny dome could be seen. They would chortle about this, but never to his face. In spite of his peculiarities, he was a good soul.

"Are there any more entrants for the longest feather contest?" boomed his voice through a hand-held megaphone. The judges looked about the crowd. There was, again, a general buzz within the crowd. They all looked at each other, waiting to see if any one came forward.

"Here," shouted three voices from the back of the throng. Mickey, Stu and Breathe pushed forward with Othello leading the way, her nose acting as a prod. They moved in unison. Again, a general mumble came from the crowd. There were also sporadic cheers and a few shouts of "atta boy!" around them. A few people patted them on their backs as they forged their way to the front.

"Make way. Let 'em through. Give the kids a break," Mr. Walser said. The push through became easier as the people parted, creating a path for the children, and then closed up rapidly.

"Mr. Walser," said Mickey in a tone that was reminiscent of his father. He extended his hand, which carried the feather. There were a lot oohs and ahhhs from the observers. "Here's the feather that I want entered into the contest," he boasted, with Stu and Breathe nodding in agreement.

Mr. Walser accepted the feather. One of the other judges— James Collins, the city attorney—placed a measuring tape alongside the feather. The three judges looked on. They re-measured it and talked among themselves.

Twenty-three and three-eighths inches," cried James. There was great cheering from the crowd. This feather not only was the longest ever entered into the contest, but, it could have been the longest feather ever captured in the state.

"Mickey, what proof do you have that you shot the pheasant that was the owner of this fine feather?" asked the third judge as he smiled and looked out across the horde of onlookers. Mickey and the other two looked at each other and then downward.

"Mr. Walser, I did not shoot no pheasant," Mickey said. "We had planned on hunting pheasants, but our plans got changed at the last minute, as you all well know." He went on to explain how he'd lost his gun and how they had come across the pheasants, and how they had found the feather floating atop the beards of grain.

"Well, I'm sorry to inform you, but the rules state that you must provide the dead carcass of the bird where you got the feather. Rules are rules," said Mr. Walser as he pointed his finger at the three.

The crowd responded with boos and jeers. They shook their fists at the judges. Othello became irritated at the noise and began barking and barking. The crowd moved forward en masse, as if to threaten the judges.

"Where does it say in the rules about having to show the dead bird?" yelled one observer.

"Give the prize to Mickey!" cried another.

"Shame on you for stealing from the boy!" said someone else. The crowd grew more restless. The judges took a step back. James Collins motioned to the other two judges to go inside.

James had been the city attorney for a very long time—over thirty years. He had a reputation in the hamlet of getting opposing sides together to resolve issues before the parties went to court. He had a way with words and a way with people. He was a consensus builder. If something had to be done in the community, James was always asked his opinion. He shunned the attention, but he was a community leader. They say he could have run for Congress, but he had no political ambitions. He had not been opposed for re-election for the past sixteen years.

"Give us a minute," said James as the two other judges and he disappeared behind the closed door of the drug store. That seemed to calm the group, and they discussed among themselves who they thought should get the prize. They did not want some outsider taking the shotgun back to the big city.

Out-of-state hunters were always a topic of discussion at any gathering spot in town. The good part was that they brought money into the town, but the negatives of strewn garbage, broken fences, hunting violations, poaching and decimated wildlife were equally important to the quiet lifestyle of the community.

The judges re-emerged from their confab and the crowd quieted in anticipation of the decision. There was tension in the air. The men folded their arms in front of their chests and the women pulled tightly on their husbands' arms. James spoke.

"Folks, we have made a decision," he said with a little wryness in his voice. The crowd gasped but continued to look at the lawyer. A big grin broke out across his thin jaw line.

"Mickey has won this year's prize for the longest feather," James announced. "I want you all to know that there is no written rule requiring a hunter to show the carcass. This was a practice started may years ago, when none of us judges were involved in the contest. So, it is only fair that—"

The roar of the crowd drowned out any further posturing from the attorney. Hats were tossed in the air and handshakes abounded.

Mickey was urged to join the judges on the stand, and he turned and gestured to Breathe and Stu to join him as well. Othello never needed an invite and was the first to join him.

Mr. Walser held the prize in hands. He raised it above his head with both hands, to the delight of the audience.

"Mickey, I am pleased to award this shotgun as the prize for the longest feather," he said. "I have just received confirmation from the state game and fish department that your feather is the longest feather *ever*."

A roaring ovation greeted the exchange of the shotgun, and there were many demands for a speech from Mickey. He looked at his mother and glanced at Breathe, who had tears streaming from her cool, blue eyes. That was priceless. Breathe never cried; at least, Mickey had never seen her cry. Stu gave her a hug and again, Mickey and Stu exchanged a knuckle handshake.

Mickey dug into his pocket and extracted his golden shield, and clutched it in his left hand. He cleared his throat and looked toward the sky, seeking help from someone. He tucked the shotgun under his right armpit and stared at the audience. It was dead quiet. The words didn't want to come out. Breathe reached out and touched his elbow. Jilly put her hands to her face.

"Thank you very much," Mickey began. "I love this town and I love all of you very much. My mom is the best, and my dog is the best. Thank you all for all you have done for my family and especially for taking care of my mom when my dad died."

The crowd erupted in a roaring ovation punctuated by whistles and "hip, hip hooray"s.

Mickey cleared his throat and rubbed his neck, then said, "I cannot accept the shotgun."

The *crowd* drew still. Mickey continued, "As much as I cherish winning the shotgun, there is a need for the money. I would like the money rather than the shotgun." He turned and gave the shotgun back to Mr. Walser.

A murmur rippled through the crowd.

Well, er, ah, we haven't ever had anyone take the money rather than the shotgun," Mr. Walser said. He dug into his pocket and pulled out a coin purse, from which he took $35. "James, Richard, dig deep, boys. Have you got some money?" The other two judges came up with the remainder of the prize money. Mr. Walser counted it, and it was all there—$100.

"Are you sure?" asked James Collins as he looked into Mickey's eyes.

"Yup. Right as rain," responded Mickey.

Richard shook Mickey's hand, and James took the money from the druggist and presented it to Mickey. The crowd applauded with approval.

"What are your plans for the money?" asked someone in the audience.

"It's for a good cause," responded Mickey as he left the stage, followed by Othello, Stu and Breathe. Many well-wishers congregated around him, extending handshakes, verbal congratulations and slaps on the back.

Mickey folded the money around his dad's badge and stuffed it into his jeans pocket.

"Let's get some ice cream. I'm famished," he said to his friends, putting his left arm around Breathe and his right around Stu. On the way out, they met Jilly and Breathe's mother.

"Are you buyin'?" Jilly inquired. They all laughed and headed toward the ice cream shop.

21

"Pleased to meet you, Mr. Richards," said Mickey as he shook hands with the owner of the town's only lumber company. "This is Breathe and Stu, my friends." Othello barked as if seeking a treat. "Oh, yes, and this is Othello."

Mr. Tom Richards greeted the three companions. "I've heard about you three," he said. "You have quite a reputation. The town is very proud of you. I hear they're planning a parade and a city picnic in your honor."

The lumberman sat in his overstuffed chair behind a sprawling, blonde-oak desk. He was delighted to be sought out by these kids. He motioned for them to sit, and leaned in toward them.

"What can I do for you today?" he asked as he folded his hands and nervously rolled his thumbs over each other. His large hands and thick fingers extended from brawny forearms, and his appendages just got thicker and blended into a massive body. He had performed physical work all his life. Tom winked at them and washed his handlebar mustache with his tongue.

"We would like to buy some lumber and paint," Mickey said with conviction in his voice. He was eager to get on with the day. "And some nails," he added.

"Well, what are you building? A doghouse?" asked Tom with wryness in his voice. He sat back in his chair. His suspenders ran down his barrel chest and down to a tapered waist. He put his hands behind his head. "How much lumber, how many gallons of paint, how many nails? Do you need a saw? Got hammers?" He stopped abruptly when he realized that the children were serious, and that his sense of humor was not funny to them. He leaned forward.

"Ok," he went on. "Tell me what you're trying to build and I'll help you figure out what supplies you need." He took out paper and pencil and looked at Mickey.

The three looked at each other. Breathe and Stu coaxed Mickey to speak up. Othello had assumed a restful posture at Breathe's feet and was not a part of this conversation.

"Go ahead, Mickey," said Breathe. "Tell him what you want to do. And maybe you need to tell him how much money you have to spend." She could be rather pushy at times, but she did have a good heart.

Tom, seeing that the trio was struggling with the meeting, arose from his chair and motioned to the group to gather at the small, round conference table adjacent to his desk. When they were seated, he spoke.

"If we're going to get anywhere, we need to trust each other. By coming in here, you have shown some trust in my company. Now is not the time to change course. So, whatever you say here stays here. A handshake is my solemn oath not to betray that trust and to accept your trust. Your handshake is a symbol of accepting my trust and giving me your trust. It is a two-way street."

He stood up and extended his hand first to Mickey, then Stu and then Breathe, and they each joined in the ceremony. Othello looked up, but then laid her head back across her front paws.

"Now, let's start with the dream castle you want to build," Tom said, sitting back down.

Mickey started. "You see, there's this run-down..."

The four of them huddled together and the words began to come forth. Mr. Richards became a co-conspirator. He wrote as fast as the three talked and often stopped them to get clarification. Their posture became animated and their laughter filled the room.

As Tom worked his way down the tally sheet, he circled each item. At the bottom, he circled and re-circled a number—*$389.28.* He went back over the numbers, not displaying them to the curious eyes of the planners. They eagerly awaited the verdict. He turned the yellow pad over and looked at them, smiling.

"I think I can fill your order within your budget of $100," he reported, and the three children burst into cheers, startling the sleeping dog. "I'll have Hank fill your order. Now, how do you plan to get these materials to your job site?" he inquired, already knowing the answer.

They had not thought of that. A panic seized them as they looked at each other. Mr. Richards broke the silence.

"For my partnership in this project and to ensure our agreement of silence, I will have Hank load and haul the supplies to your destination free of charge."

They shook hands again and clapped with excitement. Othello sat up and barked and barked. The three chattered among themselves as Tom escorted them to the front office to meet Hank.

As Tom watched them all go off together, he saw a little of his younger self in them. He shook his head, smiled to himself, and thought of the plumbing supply owner who had taken him under his wing and helped him get started in business.

*I would not be where I am today...*he thought.

22

Mickey Stellon jumped from the truck's running board and looked about. The heat from the motor took some of the coolness that swept across the rim. It was a sign of the season. The splashes of red, green, orange and tan bode of things to come. Some of the leaves had already dropped. Breathe, Stu, and Othello jumped out of the truck's box, which carried their purchase.

"It wasn't too long ago that we were here beginning our hunt for the longest feather and hoping to win the shotgun," Mickey said, and the others nodded in agreement.

Stu opined, "It's amazing how fast time flies when you're having a good time."

Time had flown. Summer was gone and autumn and its rich hues were in the air. The first week of school had come and gone. Farmers were busy reaping their harvests of grain, corn and vegetables—the forerunner of the community fall festivities that celebrated the cornucopia from which all goods flowed. Clearly, this rural town had something over big towns, and its smallness was probably the foundation.

The cool breeze made Stu's eyes water, and Breathe zipped her jacket and turned the collar up. Mickey pointed to where he wanted Hank to drop the load of supplies, and Hank said that he could get to that area without any problems. They re-boarded the supply wagon and drove toward the drop site.

The truck creaked as it jostled and rocked with every imperfection in the road, which was decreasingly defined and refined—from gravel to a two-lane path to a broken field. Mickey recognized the broken field as the same route the two thugs had taken after they'd abducted Breathe.

The delivery truck lumbered across the field, carelessly bouncing its cargo and passengers. Then, it abruptly stopped. The passengers alit and guided Hank to the predetermined drop point. The engine heaved, coughed and let out a sigh of relief as Hank shut it down.

The group formed a line at the tailgate and began pulling the load from its bed, board by board. Hank slid the box of nails to the edge and Stu latched onto it, but its weight nearly wrestled him to the ground before Mickey caught him from behind. They laughed and continued their labor of love. When the last stick was unloaded, Hank went to the delivery truck's cab and lifted a large duffle bag up from the floorboard.

"Here!" Hank said, handing the overfilled bag to Mickey. It clanked in the exchange. "Mr. Richards wants you to have these things as thanks for what you're doin.'"

Mickey unzipped the soft container and removed a hand saw, leveling string, three claw hammers, a pry bar and a two-foot bubble level. Hank returned from the cab a second time with four gallons of white paint and three paint brushes. The three ran to Hank and, much to his embarrassment, gave him a group hug, nearly toppling him and his armful of cans and brushes. They broke into what resembled a poorly formed and poorly executed square dance. They spun each other around until they were dizzy and staggering, clutching each other to keep from falling down. Othello joined in the frolic. Hank enjoyed the festivities by clapping and slapping his thighs.

"Wow," exclaimed Mickey as he wheezed, catching his breath. Breathe was bent over with her hands on her knees, supporting her upper body. Stu knelt with one knee touching the ground, fending off Othello's smooches.

"Tell Tom—er, Mr. Richards—thanks," said Stu as Hank turned toward the truck.

"Yes, thanks," echoed Breathe and Mickey as they waved to Hank.

Hank turned around and walked back to the three kids. "Tom and I go a long way back in time. We grew up together." His voice thickened. "I know he would like to hear how your project ended up," he suggested, pointing toward the rickety fence. He turned and climbed into the driver's seat, brought the engine to life and inched the truck toward the path leading to the gravel road.

Stu, Mickey and Breathe stood looking at their haul. It was like Christmas three months early.

"Best we get movin'," said Mickey, and they walked around the small cemetery, surveying what needed to be done and talking about how they might attack it. They determined that the fence could not be repaired and needed to be replaced. The wooden crosses marking the foreigners' final resting places needed mending and fresh paint as well. The excavations used by the thugs to hide their marijuana crop required bigger equipment than they had, but that was a job for a later day.

The weeds had taken control of the landscape and hidden many markers. Large divots dotted the plot where the ground had sunken over time. Tunnels had been dug by furry residents who had staked their claim to the territory.

"We have our work cut out for us," Mickey said. "Let's start by tearing out the dilapidated fence. Try to save any wood to use again."

Together, they began thrashing about the worksite. Breathe grabbed a hammer and walked toward the fence line as Mickey and Stu piled up a half dozen fence slats and carried them toward the cemetery's entrance. Othello entertained herself by sniffing out a rabbit and giving chase. Occasionally, the three would call to each other, pointing toward Othello's useless attempt to catch the more agile resident. They had their jobs and were aloof to any surroundings and to the dust cloud trailing the advancing caravan.

23

The caravan proceeded to snake its way down the winding road leading to the once-proud, once-bustling silver mining town. There had been talk of restoring the deserted hamlet as a tourist attraction, but certain factions could not agree; plus, the cost was just too prohibitive. The vehicles followed each other to a fork in the road, where they stopped and got of their units.

"Hank said he drove the kids to the cemetery and dropped them and their cargo off early this morning," said Tom Richards, motioning to the entourage to gather closer. They did so, like gangling appendages drawn by a single magnet.

"When we get to where this road draws upon the field separating the pasture from the cemetery," Tom went on, "we'll park our vehicles and walk to the cemetery. Remember, our plan is to surprise them. Cut your motors as we near the area, and coast in. And don't slam your doors. Don't be surprised if the dog spies us first."

They all mumbled in anticipation among themselves, and

with skips in their steps, re-boarded their vehicles and awaited Tom's signal to move out.

The iron horses followed in single file to the predestined launching site and coasted to a quiet halt. The riders it from their rides and gestured to each other to keep quiet by putting their index fingers to their lips. Often, giddiness overcame them and they would have to stop to regroup.

"Shhhhhhhhhh," whispered several of the trekkers as they came upon the construction camp. Sounds of pounding and sawing covered their covert footsteps and constrained their conversations. Tom pointed to the three kids and then pointed to the dog in the opposite direction. This reminded many in the group of playing hide-and-go-seek in their younger days. Was this their second childhood?

Othello's ears pricked up and she looked in their direction. She stood for the longest time, not moving; likewise did the stealthy group. It was like a stare-down at high noon on a deserted cow-town street. Who would flinch first?

Othello did. She barked with clarion alarm, alerting her three friends, as a good watchdog did.

"What is it, Othello?" Mickey asked. He had heard *that* distinct bark before. "Breathe, Stu, Othello has spotted somethin'."

Othello ran toward the hideaways, barking ferociously. She knew no fear. She raced past the three children, stunned by the clamor. They cautiously jogged far behind their guardian, looking for any sign of what aroused her.

Mickey unsnapped the restraint that secured his knife and withdrew the blade, and Stu gripped his hammer as if it were a ready weapon. Breathe had her challenge in keeping pace with the boys as her injured side began to throb, and she slowed to a walk.

"What is it, Othello? What do you see, girl?" sputtered Mickey as he battled to talk, run and inhale at the same time. Stu was off his left shoulder, keeping pace. Othello stopped abruptly, but continued to extend her throat and bounce as she barked excitedly. They reached her and secured her by the collar.

"Surprise! Surprise!" was the greeting the trio received as they advanced on the group's hideaway, unaware of the identity of the intruders. Stu picked up a rock and hurled it into the weedy area, missing any target. The three halted and called to Othello, who continued bounding toward her prey. The hair on their napes rose and a flush came over each of them. Their skin crawled and clamminess engulfed them. They looked about as whistles and war whoops greeted rang through the air.

Then, a blue baseball cap rose above the brush, and a deep voice greeted them. "What are you doin' on my land?" it boomed.

Another voice demanded, "Drop your weapons and put your hands in the air!"

And then, Othello spotted a familiar face in the bushes and sprinted toward it. She jumped on Jilly, knocking her to the dirt.

"Othello, get off of me," Jilly ordered as she lay sprawled face-down. Othello's tail was wig-wagging and she stood over Jilly, licking her face. Hank came to her rescue and Othello first growled and showed her teeth, but upon recognizing Hank, retreated and jumped up, putting her front paws on his chest.

The townspeople emerged from the thicket cheering and laughing at the three would-be carpenters. They exchanged hugs with each other as tears flowed from nearly everyone's eyes.

"What are you doing here? You nearly scared us to death," demanded Stu.

"If I were a cat, I would have a lot fewer lives," said Breathe. They laughed again and slapped each other's backs.

Before Mickey could say anything, the coughing and sputtering of the familiar lumber truck was heard approaching. The group moved to greet it and upon its lurching to a halt, they unloaded several picnic baskets. No suspicion was cast on another canvas-covered load on the far side of the truck. They were too hungry to notice, or to care.

As the men cleared an area under a shade tree, the women prepared the picnic feast. After sharing grace, they started the line, loading their plates with as much as they could hold.

"There's plenty for seconds and thirds," exclaimed Breathe's mother.

"Yes, and don't forget the June berry pies," Jilly added.

The feast was fitting for a harvest crew. First, there were homemade pickles, beets and relishes, followed by lettuce and slaw, fried chicken, hamburgers, onions, mustard, catsup, homemade mayonnaise, chilled potato salad, chips, dips, watermelon, cantaloupe and several soft drinks, including ice-cold water. Last, but not least, was the town's favorite dessert, June berry pie. Swen, the big guy, went back for seconds, asserting that he had to keep his strength up as foreman. Laughter followed.

The hubbub was overcome by munching and the compliments that always followed a great meal and dessert.

"I could use a nap," someone said as they finished their last bite. As usual, this was endorsed by many other eaters.

"Let's clean up what's left and gather around. We have a lot of work to do," said Tom. The group finished its chores and settled under the lone shade tree.

24

Tom plopped down on a fallen tree trunk in front of the assemblage. Hank took residence next to him. They surveyed the attentive group and grinned. Eye-to-eye contact forced several of the workers to look down, unable to keep a straight face.

"I was taken by your charity," Tom uttered as he looked at Mickey, Stu and Breathe. He cleared his throat, not looking at his fellow teammates. "When we met in my office and you shared what you had done with the longest feather prize, I had a pretty good idea of what you three were up to, but I wasn't sure."

He continued, "Your mother wasn't aware—Mickey, nor yours, Breathe, and Stu, not even your grams and gramps." He looked at several of the nearby folks and had to look away rapidly or get caught up in the grand emotions of the time and place.

"There is a Christmas story," Tom went on. "I can't recall the title, but it has to do with a wife and husband who are very poor and have no money for presents. The wife has long, black hair down to her waist, a prize she's coveted since childhood. The husband sells his watch to buy her combs for her hair, and she sells her hair to get money to buy his present. Sorry, I don't remember all the details."

Applause interrupted his presentation.

"We think you've kinda done the same thing," he proffered. The group stood up nodded at each other. "So we're here to help you complete your project. You are in charge. Tell us what you would want us to do."

He stood, as did Hank, and motioned for the three kids to join him up front—of course, along with Othello. She had been busy vacuuming up the spilled crumbs and searching everyone's hands.

"Speech, speech," demanded a voice from the back.

Mickey hitched his Wranglers and wiped his face. He was speechless. The crowd stood silent. He, Stu and Breathe huddled, with Othello nosing into the middle.

"I was taught to respect other people's property," Mickey began. "It's sorta like the Golden Rule. This cemetery is the final resting place for people I never knew. I learned in school about the Orientals and the hard labor they performed in the silver mines in these hills, and who knows who else—soldiers or other immigrants seeking a better life. Indians believe their burial grounds are sacred and protected by the spirits." He paused and regained his composure as Breathe embraced him with a reassuring hug. Stu nodded.

"I *would not want* my dad's final resting place to be disturbed in any way, shape or form," Mickey went on, "nor any of my family's including Mom's, Othello's and Mort's." He dug his hands deeper into his pockets. "I believe we are all stewards of all things great and small. Those resting here deserve better. So, that is why I made the choice I did. I don't even know where to start," he confessed with a deep sigh.

"Let's get on with this," said one of the workers in the crowd. "We have work to do and we're burning daylight."

Tom took the lead as foreman and began giving orders to the construction crew. They were like ants crawling across the field toward the project site. The cargo carrier lumbered close behind, although it wasn't as agile as the ants in missing the ruts and the whistle pig holes.

The crew carried out their orders with vigor, some singing and some whistling. A portable generator atop the truck began its chore as its black, snakelike cords, connected to a table saw, joined in the song. Shovels and rakes were pushing and shoving dirt back into the open pits left by the two thugs. The dust drifted across the work arena.

The smell of freshly cut wood penetrated everyone's nostrils, causing several to inhale more deeply. The old, wooden fence was ripped from it mooring and the wooden trestle above the entrance was pulled over with ropes and a pulley system. Breathe and Mickey pulled weeds from the gravestones, inventorying the names as best they could. Stu carried paint cans and brushes to a couple places along the proposed fence line.

Several hours passed with periodic rest breaks. At each interval, Tom, with Mickey at his side, gave progress reports.

The carpenters sawed and pounded. Hank employed a gas-powered auger to dig the fence-post holes and Stu was learning to mix cement. The post holes were set, and then the shovelers pushed and shoved the dirt back in the holes. A carpenter trailed behind, nailing the picket fence to the cross beams. The paint crew slopped a white coat on the bare boards, getting more on each other and the ground than on the fence.

"We're getting there," yelled the foreman. "Keep pushing. You can all rest tomorrow after church." Laughter and comments followed.

Jilly and Breathe's mother placed a new cross at the front of each grave and applied a white coat of protection to each. They eyeballed each row to ensure its straightness. They nodded to each other with approval and confirmed their work with a knuckle handshake.

The archway was erected and the ants were painting it as well. Signs of tiredness showed. The workers' minds were willing, but their muscles were not. Neck rubs were common sights and muscle rubdowns were even more apparent. A couple of the workers twisted their torsos to the left, right and all around, trying to ease the aches.

Slowly, the project neared completion. The work instruments were loaded and secured on the transporter. The cords rolled up and the paint cans were placed in double garbage bags. The hand tools were strapped into the tool crib and locked down.

"Good job, team," said the foreman, and his assistant agreed. There were handshakes and high-fives for all.

"Let's take an inspection walk around our project," encouraged Breathe as she waved for all to follow her. Othello was the point lead, trotting twenty feet ahead of the troop. They all pointed fingers at the improvements and complimented each other on their newfound talents.

"We should do this again," mused one of them. Nobody took the bait and responded.

"I would like to have a moment's silence," said Stu as he removed his baseball cap. Everyone bowed their heads, mumbled something and crossed themselves. Then, they all climbed the rear bumper of the truck, hoisted themselves into the flatbed and braced for an uncertain ride.

The truck wheezed, and a black cloud of smoke exited the exhaust pipe. The diesel tugged and pulled under the additional weight of its new passengers; it had considerably more than its original cargo to carry.

"Head 'em up," sang Tom, with the crew joining in for the "move 'em out!"

The transport entered the ingress and climbed the steep bank leading to the gravel road. Hank stopped the unit so all could look back on their deed. Nestled between two ravines was a pure, white citadel interlaced with white pickets, crosses and a huge archway. A red-, green-, yellow- and purple-striped rainbow from the billowy clouds streaked across the heavens and anchored itself beyond the ivory slats.

"Let's go," ordered Tom as he rapped on the truck's cab. The iron monster whined and growled as it gained speed. Its cargo, human and otherwise, couldn't have cared less as they nestled together, tired but pleased with what they had accomplished. Only rocks ricocheting off the truck's belly interrupted the birds' warbles.

25

Mort crept along the outer edge of Mickey's bed until he was face to face with his pal. He searched Mickey's countenance for any sign of life. A mere blink of the eye would encourage Mort to nuzzle his head against Mickey's hand, but he saw nothing. He smelled Mickey's mouth and ears, his vocal engine purring.

Mort climbed onto his buddy's bare back, incessantly kneading with his front paws as if he were preparing a bed. Mickey had all he could do to resist giggling at that crazy feline. He twitched his toes, attempting to distract the preying fur ball. Mort turned and attacked the quivering lump and clamped his sharp teeth into the movement.

"Aghhhh," yelped the sleepy head. Mickey lunged and snagged the four-legged creature by its tail. The attacker became the attacked and retaliated. It was a game they played so often.

Mort was no ordinary cat; he had personality. He followed Mickey everywhere. He was small-faced, but with a big body supported by rather long legs that betrayed his girth. Both bulging sides, accentuating a cinnamon swirl, added to his sway as he swaggered.

Jilly and Mickey had once bet on Mort's weight, with Jilly guessing the closest at twenty-one pounds. Although Othello was bigger, she had respect for Mort's swift left hook and gave him plenty of room—or, at least, tolerated him. Othello was still the boss in the house and occasionally, she had to assert her authority by chasing Mort to one of many sanctuaries.

"Mickey! Mickey, it's time to rise and shine," sang Jilly. "Today is the community fall festival. I need to get these pies there in time for the pie-judging contest. Take your shower and be sure to brush your teeth. Your breakfast is on the table."

Mickey crawled out from under the warm covers and put his feet on the cold floor. He hated that shock more than anything. It was the true wake-up call. He dashed to the bathroom and turned on the shower.

Jilly finished covering the pies. She placed her hands on her hips, wondering if she had forgotten anything. She checked the stove, relocked the back door and put on her windbreaker.

"Time to go! Mort, you're in charge." She tossed Mickey his jacket and opened the front door. She picked up the *Sunday Gazette*, unfolded it, and read the headline: "Two Charged in Game Warden's Death." She quickly folded the paper and laid it on the sofa. She ushered her passengers out of the house into a crisp but bright sunny day.

It was a day ordered for celebration. Jilly loaded the station wagon and drove, with Mickey and Othello, toward the city square, site of the fall festival. Othello bounded from one window to the other with her tail wig-wagging all the time.

Jilly found a parking spot under a shady tree so that if Othello needed to be incarcerated, it would at least be out of the sun. Mom and son carried their goodies to the registration desk, where they were met by several townsfolk; they greeted each other and exchanged small talk. Jilly, Mickey and Othello then moved among the crowd, causing heads to turn and inaudible conversations to erupt.

Othello loved the adulation. The other two smiled but

deflected the praise. Word of the three kids' deed had engulfed the community and had become the conversational centerpiece of the fall get-together.

"Why are they so complimentary?" asked Mickey as he shook hands and smiled back at the little girls who came up and introduced themselves. He rarely blushed, but this was the first *time* and certainly a story that would be repeated often.

"It's all part of what makes small towns so big. We may not be big in size, but we're big in heart and that makes all the difference," Jilly responded with a profound strength in her voice.

"Hey, Breathe," hollered Mickey.

"Hi, Mick," Breathe responded with excitement and an extended look into his eyes.

Jilly pretended that she did not see that look or hear the tone in Breathe's reply. "I'm going with Sally to look at the exhibits," Jilly told them. "You two stay out of trouble."

Mickey and Breathe and their escort, Othello, wandered among the townsfolk, accepting accolades from many well-wishers. They chatted when necessary, but preferred to nod and keep walking.

"Yo, Mickey, Breathe," said Stu, running toward them, wearing his same old baseball cap. "Boy, there are more people in town than I have ever seen. Where did they all come from? My gramps says there's something special happenin' here today."

"What?" Mickey asked.

"I dunno. Maybe some politician or famous person, like the person you were named after—Mick Jagger!" They laughed with delight and Mickey pulled the bill on Stu's cap down over his eyes.

"I'll roll you like a stone," Mickey quipped.

"You two!" Breathe threw her hands up in disgust and walked ahead of Mickey and Stu as they continued trip each other. "Boys are so immature, aren't they, Othello?"

The siren's blaring caught their attention. That was the clarion announcing that it was twelve o'clock noon. It was also the town's severe storm warning alert system. But, it was a special signal today. The start of the program was minutes away and it called for all to find a comfortable place from which to enjoy it.

Mickey, Stu, Breathe and Othello found their way to a spot beneath an elm tree that provided shade. They settled in to watch and listen with the other citizens.

"Ladies and gentlemen," bellowed Mayor Watson from a raised platform. "May I have your attention? We have been blessed with another bountiful harvest and you can see the graces of that gift. Please enjoy the festivities and visit each one of the booths. We have a short but very good program for you. I think you will agree. So, let's get on with it."

Cheers and whistles encouraged the mayor to expedite the program.

"We have a distinguished guest to speak to us and bestow an award today," the mayor went on. "Please help me welcome Mr. Andy Everson, regional director of the National Rifle Association. Mr. Everson."

The audience applauded politely and then quieted as the NRA executive spoke about the greatness of America's people, its land, its natural resources, its heritage and the challenges *facing* the freedom to bear arms.

Mayor Watson and Tom Richards joined Andy at center stage.

"We have a presentation to make," boomed Tom. He pointed to a table hidden partially by the speaker's podium. The crowd hushed. "Rather, we have three presentations to make. There is no one better to make these presentations than our honored guest from the east, Andy Everson. Andy, it's all yours."

Andy moved to the center of the stage as Tom and the mayor took backseats.

"You have, right here in your own community, what I just spoke about, people-the greatest of all assets, its people," Andy said. "Regardless of your political beliefs, our anchors *are in* the past and our footprints lead to the future, and our Constitution of the United States and the Bill of Rights are our freedom's foundation."

The crowd's bosom swelled with pride, resulting in a standing ovation complemented by whistles and cheers.

"Is Mickey Stellon here?" Andy then asked. The crowd searched for him, and several folks pointed in his direction. Mickey struggled to his feet, embarrassed by the recognition. He blushed as Breathe and Stu pushed him, speeding up his saunter forward.

"Is Breathe Harper here?" Andy asked, and the crowd pointed in her direction. She robotically stumbled toward the stage as if someone else were moving her legs. She buried her face in her hands, hiding her embarrassment.

"How 'bout Stu Miller?" Andy said at last. Mickey and Breathe waved to Stu, encouraging him to join them onstage. Stu pulled his cap down low on his forehead, as if to hide his eyes, and moseyed to join his comrades. Of course, Othello was not to be left out, and she sprinted to the stage ahead of Stu, encouraged by the cheers of the onlookers.

Andy then motioned Jilly in the audience. She moved toward the stage's edge and climbed the steps with assistance from a gentleman's hand. She continued across the stage until she stood next to her son. Andy motioned to Breathe's mother as well, who followed the same path as Jilly and went up to stand next to her daughter.

Andy then looked out over the people until his eyes made contact with an elderly, Oriental gentleman sitting in a wheel-chair—Stu's grandfather, and the oldest citizen in the valley. Andy wheeled Gramps to the stage's steps and, with the aid of two burly bystanders, lifted the two-wheeled contraption and its rider onto the stage, parking both next to his only grandson.

Tom cleared his throat. "Fellow citizens," he announced, "By now, you know of the noble acts of courage, valor and citizenship these three young people performed recently. I am not going to retell their stories. That is for each of them to do. Instead, we are taking this time to honor each of them and thank them for their bravery, and for setting an example for all of us—young or otherwise."

As the crowd laughed and clapped in approval, Tom turned toward the surprised honorees. "This moment is ours, but the memories are yours. Your story will be retold over time by others, and will grow beyond its truth. That is what legends are, and you are what heroes are made of, and when we have no heroes, the legends certainly will die."

The mayor, Andy and Tom exchanged places on the stage. The mayor took the lead and unrolled a piece of scrolled paper.

"Mickey Stellon, on behalf of the citizens and the mayor's office, it is my supreme honor to present you with this key to the city for acts of courage and citizenship." He withdrew a red-, white- and blue-striped ribbon, with a large, gold, skeleton key hanging from it, from a blue, velvet box. He faced Mickey and shook his hand, and then placed the award around Mickey's neck. He also shook Jilly's hand and kissed her on the cheek as tears flowed from her eyes. He repeated the presentation with Breathe and her mother and Stu and his grandfather. The ovation was thunderous, causing Othello to bark and bark and bark.

Andy stepped to the podium and nodded at the guests and the crowd. "I'm going to make this short and sweet," he said. "I see some good pies and cakes out there, and we all would rather eat than listen to me. So, we have one more thing left to do." He turned and nodded at Tom, and the mayor carried a small table with a cover over it to center stage.

"Mickey, we all know that you took cash rather than the shotgun," Andy went on. "No one could understand it, but you did." He motioned to the two caretakers. Tom pulled a long object from under the canvas, placed it on the table, and unwrapped it.

Andy continued, "We know how much your heart was set on winning a new shotgun, after seeing the condition of your old shotgun." Tom slid Mickey's old shotgun from its hold and displayed it above his head for all to see. It looked more like an ancient war club, as the stock was broken in half and the barrel had a downward bend in it.

Mickey broke into a broad smile. "That's my gun. Where did they find it?" he whispered to his mother.

"Shhhhhhh," she responded with a touch on his arm.

"Mickey, we want you to enjoy your bird hunting in the valley for years to come," said the mayor as Tom pulled out a brand-new shotgun from under the canvas. Tom beckoned Mickey forward, and Mickey obliged with a gentle nudge from his mom. Tom read from etched inscription on the side of the shotgun: "The Longest Feather." Then, he turned the gun and read from the etching on the other side: "The Tallest Tale." He then presented the shotgun to Mickey.

"Breathe, we hear you have an interest hunting as well," said Andy as Tom pulled another shotgun from under the canvas and calling Breathe forward. Tears flowed down her high cheeks and over her smiling lips. Andy read the same inscriptions from both sides of her gift, and then presented the shotgun to Breathe.

"Stu, the birds do not stand a chance with you now," said Andy, and Tom pulled the third identical shotgun from under the canvas and started to call Stu forward—but Stu was already standing in front of them. The crowd roared with delight. Andy read the third identical etchings and presented the shotgun to Stu, who danced around the stage with his new partner. Again, the crowd roared its approval.

Andy put his arms out, calling for silence. "Now, here's a story about he longest feather and the tallest tale. A state record for the longest pheasant feather, and the tallest tale for who would ever believe either story," he quipped. "Look for this write-up in tomorrow's paper."

"Hold on there," he said. "We nearly forgot one more of our finest citizens."

The audience stopped to hear more. Tom went on, "Othello, we would never leave you out, nor would you ever let us." He chuckled as he called her forward. She came with a bound. He placed a patriotic ribbon around her neck, with a talisman of twisted rawhide bone. From under the canvas, he withdrew a bright yellow collar with a riveted silver plate. Tom held the collar up for all to see and then read the inscription: "The Longest Feather/The Longest Tale." He stooped and attached the new collar around Othello's neck and patted her on the head. Her tail wig-wagged.

Then, he stood up straight and said, "Let's have some dessert—a lot of dessert!"

The crowd filtered into the Main Street square, visiting and cajoling. The honored guests and dignitaries continued to chat onstage and admire the three identical shotguns. Othello had moved to one side and began enjoying *her* "key to the city."

26

As the sun set on the community rooftops, the autumn coolness invaded the landscape and forecasted events to come. There was always great excitement in the community as it prepared for the fall fest and then—suddenly—it was over too soon.

In past years, the vendors hurriedly dismantled their displays, packed their offerings and left the community. The townsfolk also left for their homes in much haste, to prepare for the following day.

But there was something different this year. The visitors and residents stood around and visited as if none of them wanted the day to expire. The day's events were told and retold. Already the kids' escapades were being embellished. There were three thugs—or was it four? Were the children were captured and then escaped. Did Othello *chase* the bad guys away?

As dusk appeared, shadows crept upward on the facades of Main Street. Mickey, Breathe and Stu strolled along as they headed to their homes, recounting their day of fame. Their silhouettes cast larger-than-life shadows on the storefront windows. They were energized but exhausted. Othello trailed behind them as if she were feeling the effects of the day, but from the ravaged state of her "key to the city," it was clear that she had enjoyed it.

"She's such a pretty girl and her new yellow collar shows her off," boasted Mickey as he slapped his hand against his thigh, encouraging Othello to hasten the pace. She responded by heeling.

"We need to get you a bright bandana to go with your new collar," said Breathe, rubbing Othello's ears. "We girls need to stick together. I know just the one."

"How 'bout me?" joked Stu as he took Breathe's hands and tried to place them on his ears. She pushed him away, and they all laughed.

They came upon a hopscotch diagram and each tripped lightly through its maze, except for Othello. They stopped to read some of the children's chalk writings and diagrams. Breathe picked up a red piece of chalk and drew a large heart and scratched their four initials within its confines, using "O" for their four-legged companion. Mickey took the chalk and wrote "M" alongside the "O." Then, they skipped along the sidewalk, kicking a tin can ahead of them as well as any occasional rocks that got in their way.

"Don't step on a crack or you'll break your mother's back," challenged Stu, and so they danced to avoid the cracks in the sidewalk until they came to the corner that signaled the splitting of their path—at least for the time being. Breathe hugged and kissed both of the young men and stroked Othello's back.

They stood at the corner as if waiting for the traffic to pass by, but there were no cars coming or going. They fidgeted, none of them wanting to be the first to break company. They tried small talk, but it faltered.

"What are we going to do for excitement next?" asked Breathe.

"I dunno," said Stu.

The three of them shrugged. Othello saved the moment by

pushing her nose into Mickey's backside, suggesting that it was time to go. Mickey seized the opportunity to ease the discomfort they all felt.

"Are you hungry, girl?" he asked the dog weakly. He looked at Breathe, and then at Stu, and then back at Breathe. He took her hand and squeezed it twice. He shook Stu's hand, then reached forward with his left hand and cupped Stu's left elbow.

"Come on, Othello." Mickey patted his thigh, encouraging her to heel. He stepped into the street and turned back to see Stu and Breathe one more time, and they were doing the same as they started on their separate ways home. They all smiled at each other and waved, knowing that their lives would never be the same. They had formed a bond that no one could ever dissolve.

"Peace," toasted Stu as he held his hand up, two fingers in a V. The other two responded in kind, and then each embarked in solitude.

27

As Mickey opened the front door, he was greeted by the rest of his family: Mom and Mort. Jilly greeted him with a robust hug.

"I am so proud of you, and I know your father would be as well," She said, handing him a long box wrapped in colored tissue paper. "This is for you, from me. I think you'll like it." She watched him carefully untie the bow and separate the paper from its box.

"Wow," Mickey exclaimed as he gazed at his mother's gift.

It was a wooden box with a glass cover that housed the prize-winning longest feather. He recognized the handwriting on a note within the case and read it aloud:

This may be the longest feather and the tallest tale,
but you will always be my son.
Whether you succeed or whether you fail.
Love, Mom

He knew just the place for it, but for now, he just cradled it against his chest and smiled.